It was true. She was the mother of *triplets*.

"So, what's our plan for getting back our marriage license?" she asked. "I guess we can just drive out to Brewer first thing in the morning and ask for it back. If we get to the courthouse early and spring on them the minute they open, I'm sure we'll get the license back before it's processed."

"Sounds good," he said.

"And if we can't get it back for whatever reason, we'll just have to get the marriage annulled."

"Like it never happened," he said.

"Exactly," she said with a nod and smile.

Except it had happened, and Reed had a feeling he wouldn't shake it off so easily, even with an annulment and the passage of time. The pair of them had gotten themselves into a real pickle, as his grandmother used to say.

* * *

THE WYOMING MULTIPLES:
Lots of babies, lots of love

Dear Reader,

In my series The Wyoming Multiples, a century-old wedding chapel has a legend attached to it: those who marry there will have multiples—twins, triplets, quadruplets, even quintuplets in three cases—in some way, whether through luck, science, marriage or happenstance.

Single mother of seven-month-old triplets Norah Ingalls doesn't believe in legends; after all, she *didn't* marry in the chapel and boom: triplets, two girls and a boy. But then one summer evening, she *does* marry in the chapel under the strangest circumstances, and that's how the legend comes true (belatedly) not only for her but for confirmed bachelor Detective Reed Barelli...

Did you know that I also recently wrote six novels in the Hurley's Homestyle Kitchen series for Special Edition under the pen name Meg Maxwell? For more information about me and my books, please visit my website, melissasenate.com. You can also write me with comments or questions at MelissaSenate@yahoo.com, friend me on Facebook at Facebook.com/MelissaSenate and follow me on Twitter at Twitter.com/MelissaSenate. I love to hear from readers.

Thanks so much for your interest in *The Detective's Legendary Triplets*. I hope you enjoy it!

Thank you!

Melissa Senate

Detective Barelli's Legendary Triplets

Melissa Senate

HARLEQUIN® SPECIAL EDITION

Recycling programs
for this product may
not exist in your area.

ISBN-13: 978-1-335-46585-6

Detective Barelli's Legendary Triplets

Copyright © 2018 by Melissa Senate

Printed in U.S.A.

Melissa Senate has written many novels for Harlequin and other publishers, including her debut, *See Jane Date*, which was made into a TV movie. She also wrote seven books for Harlequin's Special Edition line under the pen name Meg Maxwell. Her novels have been published in over twenty-five countries. Melissa lives on the coast of Maine with her teenaged son, their sweet rescue Shepherd mix, Flash, and a lap cat named Cleo. For more information, please visit her website, melissasenate.com.

Dedicated to my darling Max.

Chapter One

The first thing Norah Ingalls noticed when she woke up Sunday morning was the gold wedding band on her left hand.

Norah was not married. Had never been married. She was as single as single got. With seven-month-old triplets.

The second thing was the foggy headache pressing at her temples.

The third thing was the very good-looking stranger lying next to her.

A memory poked at her before panic could even bother setting in. Norah lay very still, her heart just beginning to pound, and looked over at him. He had short, thick, dark hair and a hint of five-o'clock shadow along his jawline. A scar above his left eyebrow. He was on his back, her blue-and-white quilt half covering him down by his belly button. An innie. He had an impressive six-pack. Very little chest hair. His biceps and triceps were something to behold. The man clearly worked out. Or was a rancher.

Norah bolted upright. Oh God. Oh God. Oh God. He wasn't a rancher. He was a secret service agent! She remembered now. Yes. They'd met at the Wedlock Creek Founder's Day carnival last night and—

And had said no real names, no real stories, no real anything. A fantasy for the night. That had been her idea. She'd insisted, actually.

The man in her bed was not a secret service agent. She had no idea who or what he was.

She swallowed against the lump in her parched throat.

She squeezed her eyes shut. What happened? *Think, Norah!*

There'd been lots of orange punch. And giggling, when Norah was not a giggler. The man had said something about how the punch must be spiked.

Norah bit her lower lip hard and looked for the man's left hand. It was under the quilt. Her grandmother's hand-me-down quilt.

She sucked in a breath and peeled back the quilt enough to reveal his hand. The same gold band glinted on his ring finger.

As flashes of memories from the night before started shoving into her aching head, Norah eased back down, lay very still and hoped the man wouldn't wake before she remembered how she'd ended up married to a total stranger. The fireworks display had started behind the Wedlock Creek chapel and everything between her and the man had exploded, too. Norah closed her eyes and let it all come flooding back.

A silent tester burst of the fireworks display, red and white just visible through the treetops, started when she and Fabio were on their tenth cup of punch at the carnival. The big silver punch bowl had been on an unmanned table near the food booths. Next to the stack of plastic cups was a lockbox with a slot and a sign atop it: Two Dollars A Cup/Honor System. Fabio had put a hundred-dollar bill in the box and taken the bowl and their cups under a maple tree, where they'd been sitting for the past half hour, enjoying their punch and talking utter nonsense.

Not an hour earlier Norah's mother and aunt Cheyenne had insisted she go enjoy the carnival and that they'd babysit the triplets. She'd had a corn dog, won a little stuffed dolphin in a balloon-dart game, which she'd promptly lost somewhere, and then had met the very handsome newcomer to town at the punch table.

"Punch?" he'd said, handing her a cup and putting a five-dollar bill in the box. He'd then ladled himself a cup.

She drank it down. Delicious. She put five dollars in herself and ladled them both two more cups.

"Never seen you before," she said, daring a glance up and down his six-foot-plus frame. Muscular and lanky at the same time. Navy Henley and worn jeans and cowboy boots. Silky, dark hair and dark eyes. She could look, but she'd never touch. No sirree.

He extended his hand. "I'm—"

She held up her own, palm facing him. "Nope. No real names. No real stories." She was on her own tonight, rarely had a moment to herself, and if she was going to talk to a man, a handsome, sexy, no-ring-on-his-finger man—something she'd avoided since becoming a mother—a little fantasy was in order. Norah didn't date and had zero interest in romance. Her mother, aunt and sister always shook their heads at that and tried to remind her that her faith in love, and maybe herself, had been shaken, that was all, and she'd come around. That was all? Ha. She was done with men with a capital *D*.

He smiled, his dark brown eyes crinkling at the corners. Early thirties, she thought. And handsome as sin. "In that case, I'm…Fabio. A…secret service agent. That's right. Fabio the secret service agent. Protecting the fresh air here in Wedlock Creek."

She giggled for way too long at that one. Jeez, was there something in the punch? Had to be. When was the last time she'd giggled? "Kind of casually dressed for a Fed," she pointed out, admiring his scuffed brown boots.

"Gotta blend," he said, waving his arm at the throngs of people out enjoying the carnival.

"Ah, that makes sense. Well, I'm Angelina, international flight attendant." Where had *that* come from? Angelina had a sexy ring to it, she thought. She picked up a limp fry from the plate he'd gotten from the burger booth across the field. She dabbed it in the ketchup on the side and dangled it in her mouth.

"You manage to make that sexy," he said with a grin.

Norah Ingalls, single mother of drooling, teething triplets, sexy? LOL. Ha. That was a scream. She giggled again and he tipped up her face and looked into her eyes.

Kiss me, you fool, she thought. *You Fabio. You secret service agent.* But his gaze was soft on her, not full of lascivious intent. Darn.

That was when he suggested they sit, gestured at the maple tree, then put the hundred in the lockbox and took the bowl over to their spot. She carried their cups.

"Have more punch," she said, ladling him a cup. And another. And another. He told her stories from his childhood, mostly about an old falling-down ranch on a hundred acres, but she wasn't sure what was true and what wasn't. She told him about her dad, who'd been her biggest champion. She told him the secret recipe for her mother's chicken pot pie, which was so renowned in Wedlock Creek and surrounding towns that the *Gazette* had done an article on her family's pie diner. She told him everything but the most vital truth about herself.

Tonight, Norah was a woman out having fun at the annual carnival, allowing herself for just pumpkin-hours to bask in the attention of a good-looking, sexy man who was sweet and smart and funny as hell. At midnight—well, 11:00 p.m. when the carnival closed—she'd turn back into herself. A woman who didn't talk to hot, single men.

"What do you think the punch is spiked with?" she

asked as he fed her a cold french fry and poured her another cup.

He ran two fingers gently down the side of her cheek. "I don't know, but it sure is nice to forget myself, just for a night when I'm not on duty."

Duty? *Oh, right*, she thought. He was a secret service agent. She giggled, then sobered for a second, a poke of real life jabbing at her from somewhere.

Now the first booms of the fireworks were coming fast and there were cheers and claps in the distance, but they couldn't see the show from their spot.

"Let's go see!" she said, taking his hand to pull him up.

But Fabio's expression had changed. He seemed lost in thought, far away.

"Fabio?" she asked, trying to think through the haze. "You okay?"

He downed another cup of punch. "Those were fireworks," he said, color coming back into his face. "Not gunfire."

She laughed. "Gunfire? In Wedlock Creek? There's no hunting within town limits because of the tourism and there hasn't been a murder in over seventy years. Plus, if you crane your neck, you can see a bit of the fireworks past the trees."

He craned that beautiful neck, his shoulder leaning against hers. "Okay. Let's go see."

They walked hand in hand to the chapel, but by the time they got there—a few missed turns on the path due to their tipsiness—the fireworks display was over.

The small group setting them off had already left the dock, folks clearing away back to the festival.

The Wedlock Creek chapel was all lit up, the river behind it illuminated by the glow of the almost full moon.

"I always dreamed of getting married here," she said, gazing up at the beautiful white-clapboard building, which looked a bit like a wedding cake. It had a vintage Victorian look with scallops on the upper tiers and a bell at the top that almost looked like a heart. According to town legend, those who married here would—whether through marriage, adoption, luck, science or happenstance—be blessed with multiples: twins or triplets or even quadruplets. So far, no quintuplets. The town and county was packed with multiples of those who'd gotten married at the chapel, proof the legend was true.

For some people, like Norah, you could have triplets and not have stepped foot in the chapel. Back when she'd first found out she was pregnant, before she'd told the baby's father, she'd fantasized about getting married at the chapel, that maybe they'd get lucky and have multiples even if it was "after the fact." One baby would be blessing enough. Two, three, even four—Norah loved babies and had always wanted a houseful. But the guy who'd gotten her pregnant, in town on the rodeo circuit, had said, "Sorry, I didn't sign up for that," and left town before his next event. She'd never seen him again.

She stared at the chapel, so pretty in the moonlight, real life jabbing her in the heart again. *Where is that punch bowl?* she wondered.

"You always wanted to marry here? Then let's get married," Fabio said, scooping her up and carrying her into the chapel.

Her laughter floated on the summer evening breeze. "But we're three sheets to the wind, as my daddy used to say."

"That's the only way I'd get hitched," he said, slurring the words.

"Lead the way, cowboy." She let her head drop back.

Annie Potterowski, the elderly chapel caretaker, local lore lecturer and wedding officiant, poked her head out of the back room. She stared at Norah for a moment, then her gaze moved up to Fabio's handsome face. "Ah, Detective Barelli! Nice to see you again."

"You know Fabio?" Norah asked, confused. Or was his first name really Detective?

"I ran into the chief when he was showing Detective Barelli around town," Annie said. "The chief's my second cousin on my mother's side."

Say that five times fast, Norah thought, her head beginning to spin.

And Annie knew her fantasy man. Her fantasy groom! *Isn't that something*, Norah thought, her mind going in ten directions. Suddenly the faces of her triplets pushed into the forefront of her brain and she frowned. Her babies! She should be getting home. Except she felt so good in his arms, being carried like she was someone's love, someone's bride-to-be.

Annie's husband, Abe, came out, his blue bow tie a bit crooked. He straightened it. "We've married sixteen couples tonight. One pair came as far as Texas to get hitched here."

"We're here to be the seventeenth," Fabio said, his arm heavy around Norah's.

"Aren't you a saint!" Annie said, beaming at him. "Oh, Norah, I'm so happy for you."

Saint Fabio, Norah thought and burst into laughter. "Want to know a secret?" Norah whispered into her impending husband's ear as he set her on the red velvet carpet that created an aisle to the altar.

"Yes," he said.

"My name isn't really Angelina. It's Norah. With an *h*."

He smiled. "Mine's not Fabio. It's Reed. Two *e*'s." He staggered a bit.

The man was as tipsy as she was.

"I never thought I'd marry a secret service agent," she said as they headed down the aisle to the "Wedding March."

"And we could use all your frequent flyer miles for our honeymoon," Reed added, and they burst into laughter.

"Sign here, folks," Annie said as they stood at the altar. The woman pointed to the marriage license. Norah signed, then Reed, and Annie folded it up and put it in an addressed, stamped envelope.

I'm getting married! Norah thought, gazing into Reed's dark eyes as he stood across from her, holding her hands. She glanced down at herself, confused by her shorts and blue-and-white T-shirt. Where was her strapless, lace, princess gown with the beading and sweetheart neckline she'd fantasized about from watching *Say Yes to the Dress*? And should she be getting married in her beat-up slip-on sneakers? They were hardly white anymore.

But there was no time to change. Nope. Annie was already asking Reed to repeat his vows and she wanted to pay attention.

"Do you, Reed Barelli, take this woman, Norah Ingalls, to be your lawfully wedded wife, for richer and for poorer, in sickness and in health, till death do you part?"

"I most certainly do," he said, then hooted in laughter.

Norah cracked up, too. Reed had the most marvelous laugh.

Annie turned to Norah. She repeated her vows. Yes, God, yes, she took this man to be her lawfully wedded husband.

"By the power vested in me by the State of Wyoming, I now pronounce you husband and wife! You may kiss your bride."

Reed stared at Norah for a moment, then put his hands on either side of her face and kissed her, so tenderly, yet passionately, that for a second, Norah's mind cleared completely and all she felt was his love. Her new husband of five seconds, whom she'd known for about two hours, truly loved her!

Warmth flooded her, and when rice, which she realized Abe was throwing, rained down on them, she giggled, drunk as a skunk.

Reed Barelli registered his headache before he opened his eyes, the morning sun shining through the sheer white curtains at the window. Were those embroidered flowers? he wondered as he rubbed his aching temples. Reed had bought a bunch of stuff for his new house yesterday afternoon—everything from down pillows to coffee mugs to a coffee maker itself, but he couldn't remember those frilly curtains. They weren't something he'd buy for his place.

He fully opened his eyes, his gaze landing on a stack of books on the bedside table. A mystery. A travel guide to Wyoming. And *Your Baby's First Year*.

Your Baby's First Year? Huh?

Wait a minute. He bolted up. Where the hell was he? This wasn't the house he'd rented.

He heard a soft sigh come from beside him and turned to the left, eyes widening.

Holy hell. There was a woman sleeping in his bed.

More like he was in *her* bed, from the looks of the place. He moved her long reddish-brown hair out of her face and closed his eyes. Oh Lord. Oh no. It was her—Angelina slash Norah. Last night he'd given in to her game of fantasy, glad for a night to eradicate his years as a Cheyenne cop.

He blinked twice to clear his head. He wasn't a Cheyenne cop anymore. His last case had done him in and, after a three-week leave, he'd made up his mind and gotten himself a job as a detective in Wedlock Creek, the idyllic town where he'd spent several summers as a kid with his maternal grandmother. A town where it seemed nothing could go wrong. A town that hadn't seen a murder in over seventy years. Hadn't Norah mentioned that last night?

Norah. Last night.

He lifted his hand to scrub over his face and that was when he saw it—the gold ring on his left hand. Ring finger. A ring that hadn't been there before he'd gone to the carnival.

What the...?

Slowly, bits and pieces of the evening came back to him. The festival. A punch bowl he'd commandeered into the clearing under a big tree so he and Norah could have the rest of it all to themselves. A clearly heavily *spiked* punch bowl. A hundred-dollar bill in the till, not to mention at least sixty in cash. Norah, taking his hand and leading him to the chapel.

She'd always dreamed of getting married, she'd said.

And he'd said, "Then let's get married."

He'd said that! Reed Barelli had uttered those words!

He held his breath and gently peeled the blue-and-white quilt from her shoulder to look at her left hand—which she used to yank the quilt back up, wrinkling her cute nose and turning over.

There was a gold band on her finger, too.

Holy moly. They'd really done it. They'd gotten married?

No. Couldn't be. The officiant of the chapel had called him by name. Yes, the elderly woman had known him, said she'd seen the chief showing him around town yesterday when he'd arrived. And she'd seemed familiar with Norah, too. She knew both of them. She wouldn't let them drunk-marry! That was the height of irresponsible. And as a man of the law, he would demand she explain herself and simply undo whatever it was they'd

Chapter Two

"I'm sure we're not really married!" Norah said on a high-pitched squeak, the top sheet wrapped around her as she stood—completely freaked out—against the wall of her bedroom, staring at the strange man in her bed.

A man who, according to the wedding ring on her left hand—and the one on his—*was* her husband.

She'd pretended to be asleep when he'd first started stirring. He'd bolted upright and she could feel him staring at her. She couldn't just lie there and pretend to be asleep any longer, even if she was afraid to open her eyes and face the music.

But a thought burst into her brain and she'd sat up, too: she'd forgotten to pick up the triplets. As her aunt's words had come back to her, that Cheyenne didn't expect her to pick up the babies last night, that she'd take signed. Dimly, he recalled the marriage license, scrawling his name with a blue pen.

Norah stirred. She was still asleep. For a second he couldn't help but stare at her pretty face. She had a pale complexion, delicate features and hazel eyes, if he remembered correctly.

If they'd made love, *that* he couldn't remember. And he would remember, drunk to high heaven or not. What had been in that punch?

Maybe they'd come back to her place and passed out in bed?

He closed his eyes again and slowly opened them. *Deep breaths, Barelli.* He looked around the bedroom to orient himself, ground himself.

And that was when he saw the framed photograph on the end table on Norah's side. Norah in a hospital bed, in one of those thin blue gowns, holding three newborns against her chest.

Ooh boy.

them to the diner this morning, Norah had calmed down. And slowly had opened her eyes. The sight of the stranger awake and staring at her had her leaping out of bed, taking the sheet with her. She was in a camisole and underwear.

Oh God, had they…?

She stared at Reed. In her bed. "Did we?" she croaked out.

He half shrugged. "I don't know. Sorry. I don't think so, though."

"The punch was spiked?"

"Someone's idea of a joke, maybe."

"And now we're married," she said. "Ha ha."

His gaze went to the band of gold on his finger, then back at her. "I'm sure we can undo that. The couple who married us—they seemed to know both of us. Why would they have let us get married when we were so drunk?"

Now it was her turn to shrug. She'd known Annie since she was born. The woman had waitressed on and off at her family's pie diner for years to make extra cash. How could she have let Norah do such a thing? Why hadn't Annie called her mother or aunt or sister and said, *Come get Norah, she's drunk off her butt and trying to marry a total stranger*? It made no sense that Annie hadn't done just that!

"She seemed to know you, too," Norah said, wishing she had a cup of coffee. And two Tylenol.

"I spent summers in Wedlock Creek with my grandmother when I was a kid," he said. "Annie may have known my grandmother. Do the Potterowskis live near the chapel? Maybe we can head over now and get this straightened out. I'm sure Annie hasn't sent in the marriage license yet."

"Right!" Norah said, brightening, tightening the sheet around her. "We can undo this! Let's go!"

He glanced at his pile of clothes on the floor beside the bed. "I'll go into the bathroom and get dressed." He stood, wearing nothing but incredibly sexy black boxer briefs. He picked up the pile and booked into the bathroom, shutting the door.

She heard the water run, then shut off. A few minutes later the door opened and there he was, dressed like Fabio from last night.

She rushed over to her dresser, grabbed jeans and a T-shirt and fresh underwear, then sped past him into the bathroom, her heart beating like a bullet train. She quickly washed her face and brushed her teeth, got dressed and stepped back outside.

Reed was sitting in the chair in the corner, his elbows on his knees, his head in his hands. How could he look so handsome when he was so rumpled, his hair all mussed? He was slowly shaking his head as if trying to make sense of this.

"So you always wanted to be a secret service agent?" she asked to break the awkward silence.

He sat up and offered something of a smile. "I have no idea why I said that. I've always wanted to be a cop. I start at the Wedlock Creek PD on Monday. Guess you're not a flight attendant," he added.

"I've never been out of Wyoming," she said. "I bake for my family's pie diner." That was all she'd ever wanted to do. Work for the family business and perfect her savory pies, her specialty.

The diner had her thinking of real life again, Bella's, Bea's and Brody's beautiful little faces coming to mind. She missed them and needed to see them, needed to hold them. And she had to get to the diner and let her family know she was all right. She hadn't called once to check in on the triplets last night. Her mom and aunt had probably mentioned that every hour on the hour. *No call from Norah? Huh. Must be having a good time.* Then looking at each other and saying *Not* in unison, bursting into laughter and sobering up fast, wondering what could have happened to her to prevent her from calling every other minute to make sure all was well with the babies.

Her phone hadn't rung last night, so maybe they'd just thought she'd met up with old friends and was having fun. She glanced at her alarm clock on the bedside table. It was barely six o'clock. She wouldn't be expected at the diner until seven.

Reed was looking at the photo next to the clock. The one of her and her triplets taken moments after they were born. He didn't say a word, but she knew what he was thinking. Anyone would. *Help me. Get me out of this. What the hell have I done? Triplets? Ahhhhh!* She was surprised he didn't have his hands on his screaming face like the kid from the movie *Home Alone*.

Well, one thing Norah Ingalls was good at? Taking care of business. "Let's go see Annie and Abe," she said. "They wake up at the crack of dawn, so I'm sure they'll be up."

His gaze snapped back to hers. "Good idea. We can catch them before they send the marriage license into the state bureau for processing."

"Right. It's not like we're really married. I mean, it's not *legal*."

He nodded. "We could undo this before 7:00 a.m. and get back to our lives," he said.

This was definitely not her life.

Norah poked her head out the front door of her house, which, thank heavens, was blocked on both sides by big leafy trees. The last thing she needed was for all of Wedlock Creek to know a man had been spotted leaving her house at six in the morning. Norah lived around the corner from Main Street and just a few minutes' walk to the diner, but the chapel was a good half mile in the other direction.

"Let's take the parallel road so no one sees us," she said. "I'm sure you don't want to be the center of gossip before you even start your first day at the police station."

"I definitely don't," he said.

They ducked down a side street with backyards to the left and the woods and river to the right. At this early hour, no one was out yet. The Potterowskis lived in the caretaker's cottage to the right of the chapel. Norah dashed up the steps to the side door and could see eighty-one-year-old Annie in a long, pink chenille bathrobe, sitting down with tea and toast. She rang the bell.

Annie came to the door and beamed at the newlyweds. "Norah! Didn't expect to see you out and about so early. Shouldn't you be on your honeymoon?" Annie peered behind Norah and spied Reed. "Ah, there you are, handsome devil. Come on in, you two. I just made a pot of coffee."

How could the woman be so calm? Or act like their getting married was no big deal?

Norah and Reed came in but didn't sit. "Annie," Norah said, "the two of us were the victims of spiked punch at the festival last night! We were drunk out of our minds. You had to know that!"

Annie tilted her head, her short, wiry, silver curls bouncing. "Drunk? Why, I don't recall seeing you two acting all nutty and, trust me, we get our share of drunk couples and turn them away."

Norah narrowed her eyes. There was no way Annie hadn't known she was drunk out of her mind! "Annie, why would I up and marry a total stranger out of the blue? Didn't that seem weird?"

"But Reed isn't a stranger," Annie said, sipping her coffee. "I heard he was back in town to work at the PD." She turned to him. "I remember you when you were a boy. I knew your grandmother Lydia Barelli. We were dear friends from way back. Oh, how I remember her hoping you'd come live in Wedlock Creek. I suppose now you'll move to the ranch like she always dreamed."

Reed raised an eyebrow. "I've rented a house right in town. I loved my grandmother dearly, but she was trying to bribe me into getting married and starting a family. I had her number, all right." He smiled at Annie, but his chin was lifted. The detective was clearly assessing the situation.

Annie waved her hand dismissively. "Well, bribe or not, you're married. Your dear grandmother's last will and testament leaves you the ranch when you marry. So now you can take your rightful inheritance."

Norah glanced from Annie to Reed. What was all this about a ranch and an inheritance? If Reed had intended to find some drunk fool to marry to satisfy the terms and get his ranch, why would he have rented a house his first day in town?

The detective crossed his arms over his chest. "I have no intention of moving to the ranch, Annie."

"Oh, hogwash!" Annie said, waving her piece of toast. "You're married and that's it. You should move to the ranch like your grandmamma intended, and poor Norah here will have a father for the triplets."

Good golly. Watch out for little old ladies with secret agendas. Annie Potterowski had hoodwinked them both!

Norah watched Reed swallow. And felt her cheeks burn.

"Annie," Norah said, hands on hips. "You did know we were drunk! You let us marry anyway!"

"For your own good," Annie said. "Both of you. But I didn't lure you two here. I didn't spike the punch. You came in here of your own free will. I just didn't stop you."

"Can't you arrest her for this?" Norah said to Reed, narrowing her eyes at Annie again.

Annie's eyes widened. "I hope you get a chance to leave town and go somewhere exotic for your honeymoon," she said, clearly trying to change the subject from her subterfuge. "New York City maybe. Or how about Paris? It's so romantic."

Norah threw up her hands. "She actually thinks this is reasonable!"

"Annie, come on," Reed said. "We're not *really* married. A little too much spiked punch, a wedding chapel right in our path, no waiting period required—a recipe for disaster and we walked right into it. We're here to get back the marriage license. Surely you haven't sent it in."

"We'll just rip it up and be on our way," Norah said, glancing at her watch.

"Oh dear. I'm sorry, but that's impossible," Annie said. "I sent Abe to the county courthouse in Brewer about twenty minutes ago. I'm afraid your marriage license—and the sixteen others from yesterday—are well on their way to being deposited. There's a mail slot right in front of the building. Of course, it's Sunday and they're closed, so I reckon you won't be able to drive over to try to get it back."

Reed was staring at Annie with total confusion on his face. "Well, we'll have to do something at some point."

"Yeah," Norah agreed, her head spinning. Between all the spiked punch and the surprise this morning of the wedding rings, and now what appeared to be this crazy scheme of Annie's to not undo what she'd allowed to happen…

"I need coffee," Reed said, shaking his head. "A vat of coffee."

Norah nodded. "Me, too."

"Help yourself," Annie said, gesturing at the coffee-pot on the counter as she took a bite of her toast.

Reed sighed and turned to Norah. "Let's go back to your house and talk this through. We need to make a plan for how to undo this."

Norah nodded. "See you, Annie," she said as she headed to the door, despite how completely furious she was with the woman. She'd known Annie all her life and the woman had been nothing but kind to her. Annie had even brought each triplet an adorable stuffed bas-set hound, her favorite dog, when they'd been born, and had showered them with little gifts ever since.

"Oh, Norah? Reed?" Annie called as they opened the door and stepped onto the porch.

Norah turned back around.

"Congratulations," the elderly officiant said with a sheepish smile and absolute mirth glowing in her eyes.

Reed had been so fired up when he'd left Norah's house for the chapel that he hadn't realized how chilly it was this morning, barely fifty-five degrees. He glanced over at Norah; all she wore was a T-shirt and her hands were jammed in her pockets as she hunched over a bit. She was cold. He took off his jacket and slipped it around Norah's shoulders.

She started and stared down at the jacket. "Thank you," she said, slipping her arms into it and zipping it up. "I was so out of my mind before, I forgot to grab a sweater." She turned to stare at him. "Of course, now you'll be cold."

"My aching head will keep me warm," he said. "And I deserve the headache—the literal and figurative one."

"We both do," she said gently.

The breeze moved a swath of her hair in her face, the sun illuminating the red and gold highlights, and he had the urge to sweep it back, but she quickly tucked it behind her ear. "I'm a cop. It's my job to serve and protect. I had no business getting drunk, particularly at a town event."

"Well, the punch was spiked with something very strong. And you weren't on duty," she pointed out. "You're not even on the force till tomorrow."

"Still, a cop is always a cop. Unfortunately, by the time I realized the punch had to be spiked, I was too affected by it to care." He wouldn't put himself in a position like that again. Leaving Cheyenne, saying yes to Wedlock Creek—even though it meant he couldn't live in his grandmother's ranch—trying to switch off the city cop he'd been... He'd let down his guard and he'd paid for it with this crazy nonsense. So had Norah.

Damn. Back in Cheyenne, his guard had been so up he'd practically gotten himself killed during a botched stakeout. Where the hell was the happy medium? Maybe he'd never get a handle on *just right*.

"And you said you were glad to forget? Or something like that?" she asked, darting a glance at him.

He looked out over a stand of heavy trees along the side of the road. *Let it go*, he reminded himself. No rehashing, no what-ifs. "I'm here for a fresh start. Now I need a fresh start to my fresh start." He stopped and shook his head. What a mess. "Sixteen couples besides us?" he said, resuming walking. "It's a little too easy to get married in the state of Wyoming."

"Someone should change the law," Norah said. "There should be a waiting period. Blood tests required. Something, anything, so you can't get insta-married."

That was for sure. "It's like a mini Las Vegas. I wonder how many of those couples meant to get married."

"Oh, I'm sure all of them. The Wedlock Creek Wedding Chapel is famous. People come here because of the legend."

He glanced at her. "What legend?"

"Just about everyone who marries at the chapel becomes the parent of multiples in some way, shape or form. According to legend, the chapel has a special blessing on it. A barren witch cast the spell the year the chapel was built in 1895."

Reed raised an eyebrow. "A barren witch? Was she trying to be nice or up to no good?"

"No one's sure," she said with a smile. "But as the mother of triplets, I'm glad I have them."

Reed stopped walking.

She'd said it. It was absolutely true. She was the mother of *triplets*. No wonder Annie Potterowski had called him a saint last night. The elderly woman had thought he was knowingly marrying a single mother of three babies! "So you got married at the chapel?" He supposed she was divorced, though that must have been one quick marriage.

She glanced down. "No. I never did get married. The babies' father ran for the hills about an hour after I told him the news. We'd been dating for only about three months at that point. I thought we had something special, but I sure was wrong."

Her voice hitched on the word *wrong* and he took her hand. "I'm sorry." The jerk had abandoned her? She was raising baby triplets on her own? One baby seemed like a handful. Norah had three. He couldn't even imagine how hard that had to be.

She bit her lip and forced a half smile, slipping her hand away and into her pocket. "Oh, that's all right. I have my children, who I love to pieces. I have a great family, work I love. My life is good. No complaints."

"Still, your life can't be easy."

She raised an eyebrow. "Whose is? Yours?"

He laughed. "Touché. And I don't even have a pet. Or a plant for that matter."

She smiled and he was glad to see the shadow leave her eyes. "So, what's our plan for getting back our marriage license? I guess we can just drive out to Brewer first thing in the morning and ask for it back. If we get to the courthouse early and spring on them the minute they open, I'm sure we'll get the license back before it's processed."

"Sounds good," he said.

"And if we can't get it back for whatever reason, we'll just have the marriage annulled."

"Like it never happened," he said.

"Exactly," she said with a nod and smile.

Except it had happened and Reed had a feeling he wouldn't shake it off so easily, even with an annulment and the passage of time. The pair of them had gotten themselves into a real pickle as his grandmother used to say.

"So I guess this means you really didn't secretly marry me to get your hands on your grandmother's ranch," Norah said. "Between renting a house the minute you moved here yesterday and talking about annulments, that's crystal clear."

He thought about telling her why he didn't believe in marriage but just nodded instead. Last night, as he'd picked her up and carried her into that chapel, he'd been a man—Fabio the secret service agent—who *did* believe in marriage, who wanted a wife and a house full of kids. He'd liked being that guy. Of course, with the light of day and the headache and stone-cold reality, he was back to Reed Barelli, who'd seen close up that marriage wasn't for him.

Reed envisioned living alone forever, a couple of dogs to keep him company, short-term relationships with women who understood from the get-go that he wasn't looking for commitment. He'd thought the last woman he'd dated—a funny, pretty woman named Valerie was on the same page, but a few weeks into their relationship, she'd wanted more and he hadn't, and it was a mess. Crying, accusations and him saying over and over *But I told you on the first date how I felt.* That was six months ago and he hadn't dated since. He missed sex like crazy, but he wasn't interested in hurting anyone.

They walked in silence, Norah gesturing that they should cross Main Street. As they headed down Norah's street, Sycamore, he realized they'd made their plan and there was really no need for that coffee, after all. He'd walk her home and then—

"Norah! You're alive!"

Reed glanced in the direction of the voice. A young blond woman stood in front of Norah's small, white Cape Cod house, one hand waving at them and one on a stroller with three little faces peering out.

Three. Little. Faces.

Had a two-by-four come out of nowhere and whammed him upside the head?

Just about everyone who marries at the chapel becomes the parent of multiples in some way, shape or form.

Because he'd just realized that the legend of the Wedlock Creek chapel had come true for him.

Chapter Three

Norah was so relieved to see the babies that she rushed over to the porch—forgetting to shove her hand into her pocket and hide the ring that hadn't been on her finger yesterday.

And her sister, Shelby, wasn't one to miss a thing. Shelby's gaze shifted from the ring on Norah's hand to Reed and his own adorned left hand, then back to Norah. "I dropped by the diner this morning with a Greek quiche I developed last night, and Aunt Cheyenne and Mom said they hadn't heard from you. So I figured I'd walk the triplets over and make sure you were all right." She'd said it all so casually, but her gaze darted hard from the ring on Norah's hand to Norah, then back again. And again. Her sister was dying for info. That was clear.

"I'm all right," Norah said. "Everything is a little topsy-turvy, but I'm fine." She bent over and faced the stroller. "I missed you little darlings." She hadn't spent a night away from her children since they were born.

Shelby gave her throat a little faux clear. "I notice you and this gentleman are wearing matching gold wedding bands and taking walks at 6:30 a.m." Shelby slid her gaze over to Reed and then stared at Norah with her "tell me everything this instant" expression.

Norah straightened and sucked in a deep breath. Thank God her sister was here, actually. Shelby was practical and smart and would have words of wisdom.

"Reed Barelli," Norah said, "this is my sister, Shelby Mercer. Shelby, be the first to meet my accidental husband, Detective Reed Barelli of the Wedlock Creek PD...well, starting tomorrow."

Shelby's green eyes went even wider. She mouthed *What?* to Norah and then said, "Detective, would you mind keeping an eye on the triplets while my sister and I have a little chat?"

Reed eyed the stroller. "Not at all," he said, approaching warily.

Norah opened the door and Shelby pulled her inside. The moment the door closed, Shelby screeched, *"What?"*

Norah covered her face with her hands for a second, shook her head, then launched into the story. "I went to the carnival on Mom and Aunt Cheyenne's orders. The last thing I remember clearly is having a corn dog and winning a stuffed dolphin, which I lost. Then it's just flashes of the night. Reed and I drinking spiked punch—the entire bowl—and going to the chapel and getting married."

"Oh, phew," Shelby said, relief crossing her face. "I thought maybe you flew to Las Vegas or something crazy. There's no way Annie or Abe would have let you get drunk-married to some stranger. I'm sure you just *think* you got married."

"Yeah, we'd figured that, too," Norah said. "We just got back from Annie's house. Turns out she knows Reed from when he spent summers here as a kid. Apparently she was friends with his late grandmother. She called him a saint last night. Annie married us with her blessing! And our marriage license—along with sixteen others—is already at the county courthouse."

"Waaah! Waah!" came a little voice from outside.

"That sounds like Bea," Norah said. "I'd better go help—"

Shelby stuck her arm out in front of the door. "Oh no, you don't, Norah Ingalls. The man is a police officer. The babies are safe with him for a few minutes." She bit her lip. "What are you two going to do?"

Norah shrugged. "I guess if we can't get back the license before it's processed, we'll have to get an annulment."

"The whole thing is nuts," Shelby said. "Jeez, I thought my life was crazy."

Norah wouldn't have thought anything could top what Shelby had been through right before Norah had gotten pregnant. Her sister had discovered her baby and a total stranger's baby had been switched at birth six months after bringing their boys home from the Wedlock Creek Clinic. Shelby and Liam Mercer had gotten married so that they could each have both boys—and along the way they'd fallen madly in love. Now the four of them were a very happy family.

"You know what else is crazy?" Norah said, her voice going shaky. "How special it was. The ceremony, I mean. Me—even in my T-shirt and shorts and grubby slip-on sneakers—saying my vows. Hearing them said back to me. In that moment, Shel, I felt so…safe. For the first time in a year and a half, I felt safe." Tears pricked her eyes and she blinked hard.

She was the woman who didn't want love and romance. Who didn't believe in happily-ever-after anymore. So why had getting married—even to a total stranger—felt so wonderful? And yes, so safe?

"Oh, Norah," her sister said and pulled her into a hug. "I know what you mean."

Norah blew out a breath to get ahold of herself. "I know it wasn't real. But in that moment, when Annie pronounced us husband and wife, the way Reed looked at me and kissed me, being in that famed chapel…it was an old dream come true. Back to reality, though. That's just how life is."

Shelby squeezed her hand. "So, last night, did the new Mr. and Mrs. Barelli…?"

Norah felt her cheeks burn. "I don't know. But if we did, it must have been amazing. You saw the man."

Shelby smiled. "Maybe you can keep him."

Norah shook her head. Twice. "I'm done with men, remember? *Done.*"

Shelby let loose her evil smile. "Yes, for all other men, sure. Since you're married now."

Norah swallowed. But then she remembered this wasn't real and would be rectified. Brody let out a wail and once again she snapped back to reality. She was no one's bride, no one's wife. There was a big difference between old dreams and the way things really were. "I'd better go save the detective from the three little screechers."

Norah opened the door and almost gasped at the sight on the doorstep. Brody was in Reed's strong arms, the sleeves of his navy shirt rolled up. He lifted the baby high in the air, then turned to Bea and Bella in the stroller and made a funny face at them before lifting Brody again. "Upsie downsie," Reed said. "Downsie upsie," he added as he lifted Brody again.

Baby laughter exploded on the porch.

Norah stared at Reed and then glanced over at Shelby, who was looking at Reed Barelli in amazement.

"My first partner back in Cheyenne had a baby, and whenever he started fussing, I'd do that and he'd giggle," Reed explained, lifting Brody one more time for a chorus of more triplet giggles.

Bea lifted her arms. Reed put Brody back and did two upsie-downsies with Bea, then her sister.

"I'll let Mom and Aunt Cheyenne know you might not be in today," Shelby said very slowly. She glanced at Reed, positively beaming, much like Annie had done earlier. "I'll be perfectly honest and report you have a headache from the sweet punch."

"Thanks," Norah said. "I'm not quite ready to explain everything just yet."

As her sister said goodbye and walked off in the direction of the diner, Norah appreciated that Shelby hadn't added a "Welcome to the family." She turned back to Reed. He was twisting his wedding ring on his finger.

"So you were supposed to work today?" he asked.

"Yes—and Sundays are one of the busiest at the Pie Diner—but I don't think I'll be able to concentrate. My mom and aunt will be all over me with questions. And now that I think about it, with the festival and carnival continuing today, business should be slow. I'll just make my pot pies here and take them over later, once we're settled on what to say if word gets out."

"Word will get out?" he said. "Oh no—don't tell me Annie and Abe are gossips."

"They're *strategic*," Norah said. "Which is exactly how we ended up married and not sent away last night."

"Meaning they'll tell just enough people, or the right people, to make it hard for us to undo the marriage so easily."

"She probably has a third cousin at the courthouse!" Norah said, throwing up her hands. But town gossip was the least of her problems right now, and boy did she have problems, particularly the one standing across from her looking so damned hot.

She turned from the glorious sight of him and racked her brain, trying to think who she could ask to babysit this morning for a couple hours on such short notice so she could get her pies done and her equilibrium back.

Her family was out of the question, of course. Her sister was busy enough with her own two kids and her secondhand shop to run, plus she often helped out at the diner. There was Geraldina next door, who might be able to take the triplets for a couple of hours, but her neighbor was another huge gossip and maybe she'd seen the two of them return home last night in God knew what state. For all Norah knew, Reed Barelli had carried her down the street like in *An Officer and a Gentleman* and swept her over the threshold of her house.

Huh. Had he?

"You okay?" he asked, peering at her.

Her shoulders slumped. "Just trying to figure out a sitter for the triplets while I make six pot pies. The usual suspects aren't going to work out this morning."

"Consider me at your service, then," he said.

"What?" she said, shaking her head. "I couldn't ask that."

"Least I can do, Norah. I got you into this mess. If I remember correctly, last night you said you'd always wanted to get married at that chapel and I picked you up and said 'Then let's get married.'" He let out a breath. "I still can't quite get over that I did that."

"I like being able to blame it all on you. Thanks." She smiled, grateful that he was so…nice.

"Besides, and obviously, I like babies," he said, "and all I had on my agenda today was re-familiarizing myself with Wedlock Creek."

"Okay, but don't say I didn't try to let you off the hook. Triplet seven-month-olds who are just starting to crawl are pretty wily creatures."

"I've dealt with plenty of wily creatures in my eight-year career as a cop. I've got this."

She raised an eyebrow and opened the door, surprised when Reed took hold of the enormous stroller and wheeled in the babies. She wasn't much used to someone else…being there. "Didn't I hear you tell Annie that you had no intention of ever getting married? I would think that meant you had no intention of having children, either."

"Right on both counts. But I like other people's kids. And babies are irresistible. Besides, yours already adore me."

Brody was sticking up his skinny little arms, smiling at Reed, three little teeth coming up in his gummy mouth.

"See?" he said.

Norah smiled. "Point proven. I'd appreciate the help. So thank you."

Norah closed the door behind Reed. It was the strangest feeling, walking into her home with her three babies—and her brand-new husband.

She glanced at her wedding ring. Then at his.

Talk about crazy. For a man who didn't intend to marry or have kids, he now had one huge family, even if that family would dissolve tomorrow at the courthouse.

As they'd first approached Norah's house on the way back from Annie and Abe's, Reed had been all set to suggest they get in his SUV, babies and all, and find someone, anyone, to open the courthouse. They could root through the mail that had been dumped through the slot, find their license application and just tear it up. Kaput! No more marriage!

But he'd been standing right in front of Norah's door, cute little Brody in his arms, the small, baby-shampoo-smelling weight of him, when he'd heard what Norah had said. Heard it loud and clear. And something inside him had shifted.

You know what else is crazy, how special it was. The ceremony, I mean. Me—even in my T-shirt and shorts and grubby slip-on sneakers—saying my vows. Hearing them said back to me. In that moment, Shel, I felt so... safe. For the first time in a year and a half, I felt safe.

He'd looked at the baby in his arms. The two little girls in the stroller. Then he'd heard Norah say something about a dream come true and back to reality.

His heart had constricted in his chest when she'd said she'd felt safe for the first time since the triplets were born. He'd once overheard his mother say that the only time she felt safe was when Reed was away in Wedlock Creek with his paternal grandmother, knowing her boy was being fed well and looked after.

Reed's frail mother had been alone otherwise, abandoned by Reed's dad during the pregnancy, no child support, no nothing. She'd married again, more for security than love, but that had been short-lived. Not even a year. Turned out the louse couldn't stand kids. His mother had worked two jobs to make ends meet, but times had been tough and Reed had often been alone and on his own.

He hated the thought of Norah feeling that way—unsteady, unsure, alone. This beautiful woman with so much on her shoulders. Three little ones her sole responsibility. And for a moment in the chapel, wed to him, she'd felt safe.

He wanted to help her somehow. Ease her burden. Do what he could. And if that was babysitting for a couple hours while she worked, he'd be more than happy to.

She picked up two babies from the stroller, a pro at balancing them in each arm. "Will you take Bea?" she asked.

He scooped up the baby girl, who immediately grabbed his cheek and stared at him with her huge gray-blue eyes, and followed Norah into the kitchen. A playpen was wedged in a nook. She put the two babies inside and Reed put Bea beside them. They all immediately reached for the little toys.

Norah took an apron from a hook by the refrigerator. "If I were at the diner, I'd be making twelve pot pies—five chicken and three turkey, two beef, and two veggie—but I only have enough ingredients at home to do six—three chicken and three beef. I'll just make them all here and drop them off for baking. The oven in this house can't even cook a frozen pizza reliably."

Reed glanced around the run-down kitchen. It was clean and clearly had been baby-proofed, given the covered electrical outlets. But the refrigerator was strangely loud, the floor sloped and the house just seemed…old. And, he hated to say it, kind of depressing. "Have you lived here long?"

"I moved in a few months after finding out I was pregnant. I'd lived with my mom before then and she wanted me to continue living there, but I needed to grow up. I was going to be a mother—of three—and it was time to make a home. Not turn my mother into a live-in babysitter or take advantage of her generosity. This place was all I could afford. It's small and dated but clean and functional."

"So a kitchen, living room and bathroom downstairs," he said, glancing into the small living room with the gold-colored couch. Baby stuff was everywhere, from colorful foam mats to building blocks and rattling toys. There wasn't a dining room, as far as he could see. A square table was wedged in front of a window with one chair and three high chairs. "How many bedrooms upstairs?"

"Only two. But that works for now. One for me and one for the triplets." She bit her lip. "It's not a palace. It's hardly my dream home. But you do what you have to. I'm their mother and it's up to me to support us."

Everything looked rumpled, secondhand, and it probably was. The place reminded him of his apartment as a kid. His mother hadn't even had her own room. She'd slept on a pull-out couch in the living room and folded it up every morning. She'd wanted so much more for the two of them, but her paycheck had stretched only so far. When he was eighteen, he'd enrolled in the police academy and started college at night, planning to give his mother a better standard of living. But she'd passed away before he could make any of her dreams come true.

A squeal came from the playpen and he glanced over at the triplets. The little guy was chewing on a cloth book, one of the girls was pressing little "piano" keys and the other was babbling and shaking keys.

"Bea's the rabble-rouser," Norah said as she began to sauté chicken breasts in one pan, chunks of beef in another, and then set a bunch of carrots and onions on the counter. "Bella loves anything musical, and Brody is the quietest. He loves to be read to, whereas Bea will start clawing at the pages."

"Really can't be easy raising three babies. Especially on your own," he said.

"It's not. But I'll tell you, I now know what love is. I mean, I love my family. I thought I loved their father. But the way I feel about those three? Nothing I've ever experienced. I'd sacrifice anything for them."

"You're a mother," he said, admiring her more than she could know.

She nodded. "First and foremost. My family keeps trying to set me up on dates. Like any guy would say yes to a woman with seven-month-old triplets." She glanced at Reed, then began cutting up the carrots. "I sure trapped you."

He smiled. "Angelina, international flight attendant, wasn't a mother of three, remember? She was just a woman out having a good time at a small-town carnival."

She set down the knife and looked at him. "You're not angry that I didn't say anything? That I actually let you marry me without you knowing what you were walking into?"

He moved to the counter and stood across from her. "We were both bombed out of our minds."

She smiled and resumed chopping. "Well, when we

get this little matter of our marriage license ripped up before it can be processed, I'll go back to telling my family to stop trying to fix me up and you'll be solving crime all over Wedlock Creek."

"You're not looking for a father for the triplets?" he asked.

"Maybe I should be," she said. "To be fair to them. But right now? No. I have zero interest in romance and love and honestly no longer believe in happily-ever-after. I've got my hands full, anyway."

Huh. She felt the same way he did. Well, to a point. Marriage made her feel safe, but love didn't. Interesting, he thought, trying not to stare at her.

As she pulled open a cabinet, the hinge broke and it almost hit her on the head. Reed rushed over and caught it before it could.

"This place is falling down," he said, shaking his head. "You could have been really hurt. And you could have been holding one of the triplets."

She frowned. "I've fixed that three times. I'll call my landlord. She'll have it taken care of."

"Or I could take care of it right now," he said, surveying the hinge. "Still usable. Have a power drill?"

"In that drawer," she said, pointing. "I keep all the tools in there."

He found the drill and fixed the hinge, making sure it was on tight. "That should do it," he said. "Anything else need fixing?"

"Wow, he babysits *and* is handy?" She smiled at him. "I don't think there's anything else needing work," she said, adding the vegetables into a pot bubbling on the stove. "And thank you."

When the triplets started fussing, he announced it was babysitting time. He scooped up two babies and put them in Exersaucers in the living room, then raced back for the third and set Brody in one, too. The three of them happily played with the brightly colored attachments, babbling and squealing. He pulled Bea out—he knew she was Bea by her yellow shirt, whereas Bella's was orange—and did two upsie-downsies, much to the joy of the other two, who laughed and held up their arms.

"Your turn!" he said to Bella, lifting her high to the squeals of her siblings. "Now you, Brody," he added, putting Bella back and giving her brother his turn.

They sure were beautiful. All three had the same big cheeks and big, blue-gray eyes, wisps of light brown hair. They were happy, gurgling, babbling, laughing seven-month-olds.

Something squeezed in his chest again, this time a strange sensation of longing. With the way he'd always felt about marriage, he'd never have this—babies, a wife making pot pies, a family. And even in this tired old little house, playing at family felt...nicer than he expected.

Brody rubbed his eyes, which Reed recalled meant he was getting tired. Maybe it was nap time? It was barely seven-thirty in the morning, but they'd probably woken before the crack of dawn.

"How about a story?" he asked, sitting on the braided rug and grabbing a book from the coffee table. *"Lulu Goes to the Fair."* A white chicken wearing a baseball cap was on the cover. "Your mother and I went to the fair last night," he told them. "So this book will be per-fect." He read them the story of Lulu wanting to ride the Ferris wheel but not being able to reach the step until two other chickens from her school helped her. Then they rode the Ferris wheel together. The end. Bella and Brody weren't much interested in Lulu and her day at the fair, but Bea was rapt. Then they all started rubbing their eyes and fussing.

It was now eight o'clock. Maybe he'd put the babies back in the playpen to see if he could help Norah. Not that he could cook, but he could fetch.

He picked up the two girls and headed back into the kitchen, smiled at Norah, deposited the babies in the playpen and then went to get Brody.

"Thank you for watching them," she said. "And read-ing to them."

"Anytime," he said. Which felt strange. Did he mean that?

"You're sure you didn't win Uncle of the Year or something? How'd you get so good with babies?"

"Told you. I like babies. Who doesn't? I picked up a few lessons on the job, I guess."

Why had he said "anytime" though? That was kind of loaded.

With the babies set for the moment, he shook the thought from his scrambled head and watched Norah cook, impressed with her multitasking. She had six tins covered in pie crust. The aromas of the onions and chicken and beef bubbling in two big pots filled the kitchen. His stomach growled. Had they eaten break-fast? He suddenly realized they hadn't.

"I made coffee and toasted a couple of bagels," she said as if she could read his mind. She was so multi-talented, he wouldn't be surprised if she could. "I have cream cheese and butter."

"You're doing enough," he said. "I'll get it. What do you want on yours?"

"Cream cheese. And thanks."

He poured the coffee into mugs and took care of the bagels, once again so aware of her closeness, the physicality of her. He couldn't help but notice how incredibly sexy she was, standing there in her jeans and maroon T-shirt, the way both hugged her body. There wasn't anywhere to sit in the kitchen, so he stood by the counter, drinking the coffee he so desperately needed.

"The chief mentioned the Pie Diner is the place for lunch in Wedlock Creek. I'm sure I'll be eating one of those pies tomorrow."

She smiled. "Oh, good. I'll have to thank him for that. We need to attract the newcomers to town before the burger place gets 'em." She took a long sip of her coffee. "Ah, I needed that." She took another sip, then a bite of her bagel. She glanced at him as if she wanted to ask something, then resumed adding the pot pie mixtures into the tins. "You moved here for a fresh start, you said?"

He'd avoided that question earlier. He supposed he could answer without going into every detail of his life.

He sipped his coffee and nodded. "I came up for my grandmother's funeral a few months ago. She was the last of my father's family. When she passed, I suddenly wanted to be here, in Wedlock Creek, where I'd spent those good summers. After a bad stakeout a few weeks ago that almost got me killed and did get my partner injured, I'd had it. I quit the force and applied for a job in Wedlock Creek. It turns out a detective had retired just a few weeks prior."

"Sorry about your grandmother. Sounds like she was very special to you."

"She was. My father had taken off completely when I was just a month old, but my grandmother refused to lose contact with me. She sent cards and gifts and called every week and drove out to pick me up every summer for three weeks. It's a three-hour drive each way." He'd never forget being seven, ten, eleven and staring out the window of his apartment, waiting to see that old green car slowly turn up the street. And when it did, emotion would flood him to the point that it would take him a minute to rush out with his bag.

"I'm so glad you had her in your life. You never saw your dad again?"

"He sent the occasional postcard from all over the west. Last one I ever got was from somewhere in Alaska. Word came that he died and had left instructions for a sea burial. I last saw him when I was ten, when he came back for his dad's funeral—my grandfather."

"And your mom?"

"It was hard on her raising a kid alone without much money or prospects. And it was just me. She remarried, but that didn't work out well, either, for either of us." He took a long slug of the coffee. He needed to change the subject. "How do you manage three babies with two hands?"

She smiled and lay pie crust over the tins, making some kind of decoration in the center. "Same way you did bringing the triplets from the kitchen to the living room. You just have to move fast and be constantly on guard. I do what I have to. That's just the way it is."

An angry wail came from the playpen. Then another. The three Ingalls triplets began rubbing their eyes again, this time with very upset little faces.

"Perfect timing," she said. "The pies are assembled." She hurried to the sink to wash her hands, then hurried over to the playpen. "Nap time for you cuties."

"I'll help," Reed said, putting down his mug.

Brody was holding up his arms and staring at Reed. Reed smiled and picked him up, the little weight sweet in his arms. Brody reached up and grabbed Reed's cheek, like his sister had, not that there was much to grab. Norah scooped up Bea and Bella. They headed upstairs, the unlined wood steps creaky and definitely not baby-friendly when they would start to crawl, which would probably be soon.

The nursery was spare but had the basics. Three cribs, a dresser and changing table. The room was painted a pale yellow with white stars and moons stenciled all over.

"Ever changed a diaper?" she asked as she put both babies in a crib, taking off their onesies.

"Cops have done just about everything," he said. "I've changed my share of diapers." He laid the baby on the changing table. "Phew. Just wet." He made quick work of the task, sprinkling on some cornstarch powder and fastening a fresh diaper.

"His jammies are in the top drawer. Any footsie ones."

Reed picked up the baby and carried him over to the dresser, using one hand to open the drawer. The little baby clothes were very neatly folded. He pulled out the top footed onesie, blue cotton with dinosaurs. He set Brody down, then gently put his little arms and legs into the right holes, and there Brody was, all ready for bed. He held the baby against his chest, Brody's impossibly little eyes drooping, his mouth quirking.

He tried to imagine his own father holding him like this, his own flesh and blood, and just walking away. No look back. No nothing. How was it possible? Reed couldn't fathom it.

"His crib is on the right," Norah said, pointing as she took one baby girl out of the crib and changed her, then laid her down in the empty crib. She scooped up the other baby, changed her and laid her back in the crib.

He set Brody down and gave his little cheek a caress. Brody grabbed his thumb and held on.

"He sure does like you," Norah whispered.

Reed swallowed against the gushy feeling in the region of his chest. As Brody's eyes drifted closed, the tiny fist released and Reed stepped back.

Norah shut off the light and turned on a very low lullaby player. After half a second of fussing, all three babies closed their eyes, quirking their tiny mouths and stretching their arms over their heads.

"Have a good nap, my loves," Norah said, tiptoeing toward the door.

Reed followed her, his gold band glinting in the dim light of the room. He stared at the ring, then at his surroundings. He was in a nursery. With the woman he'd accidentally married. And with her triplets, whom he'd just babysat, read to and helped get to nap time.

What the hell had happened to his life? A day ago he'd been about to embark on a new beginning here in Wedlock Creek, where life had once seemed so idyllic out in the country where his grandmother had lived alone after she'd been widowed. Instead of focusing on reading the WCPD manuals and getting up to speed on open cases, he was getting his heart squeezed by three eighteen-pound tiny humans.

And their beautiful mother.

As he stepped into the hallway, the light cleared his brain. "Well, I guess I'd better get going. Pick you up at eight thirty tomorrow for the trip to Brewer? The courthouse opens at nine. Luckily, I don't report for duty until noon."

"Sounds good," she said, leading the way downstairs. "Thanks for helping. You put Brody down for his nap like a champ."

But instead of heading toward the door, he found himself just standing there. He didn't want to leave the four Ingalls alone. On their own. In this falling-down house.

He felt…responsible for them, he realized.

But he also needed to take a giant step backward and catch his breath.

So why was it so hard to walk out the door?

Chapter Four

At exactly eight thirty on Monday morning, Norah saw Reed pull up in front of her house. He must be as ready to get this marriage business taken care of as she was. Yesterday, after he'd left, she'd taken a long, hot bubble bath upstairs, ears peeled for the triplets, but they'd napped for a good hour and a half. In that time, a zillion thoughts had raced through her head, from the bits and pieces she remembered of her evening with Fabio to the wedding to waking up to find Detective Reed Barelli in her bed to how he played upsie-downsie with the triplets and read them a story. And fixed her bagel. And the cabinet.

She couldn't stop thinking about him, how kind he'd been, how good-natured about the whole mess. It had been the man's first day in town. And he'd found himself married to a mother of three. She also couldn't stop thinking about how he'd looked in those black boxer briefs, how tall and muscular he was. The way his dark eyes crinkled at the corners.

After the triplets had woken up, she'd gotten them into the stroller and moseyed on down to the Pie Diner with her six contributions. She'd been unable to keep her secret and had told her mother and aunt everything, trying to not be overheard by their part-time cook and the two waitresses coming in and out. She'd explained it all and she could see on her sister's face how relieved Shelby was at not having to keep her super-juicy family secret anymore.

"That Annie!" Aunt Cheyenne had said with a wink. "Always looking out for us."

Arlena Ingalls had had the same evil smile. "Handsome?"

"Mom!" Norah had said. "He's a stranger!"

"He's hardly that now," her mother had pointed out, glancing at an order ticket and placing two big slices of quiche Lorraine on a waitress's tray.

Aunt Cheyenne had laughed. "I have to hand it to you. We send you to the carnival for your first night out in seven months and you come home married. And to the town's new detective. I, for one, am very impressed."

After talk had turned to who had possibly spiked the punch, Norah, exasperated, had left. Her mother had offered to watch the triplets this morning so that Norah could get her life straightened out and back together. "If you absolutely have to," her mother had added.

Humph, Norah thought now, watching Reed get out

of his dark blue SUV. As if marriage was the be-all and end-all. As if a good man was a savior. They didn't even know if Reed was a good man.

But she did, dammit. That had been obvious from the get-go, from the moment he'd stuffed that hundred in the till box to pay what he'd thought was fair for swiping all the punch to picking her up and taking her into the chapel to fulfill her dream of getting married there. He was a good man when bombed out of his ever-loving mind. He was a good man stone-cold sober, who played upsie-downsie with babies, making sure each got their turn. He'd fixed her broken cabinet.

And damn, he really was something to look at. His thick, dark hair shone in the morning sun. He wore charcoal-colored pants, a gray button-down shirt and black shoes. He looked like a city detective.

In the bathtub, as she'd lain there soaking, and all last night in bed, in between trips to the nursery to see why one triplet or another was crying or shrieking, she'd thought about Reed Barelli and how he'd looked in those boxer briefs. She was pretty sure they hadn't had sex. She would remember, wouldn't she? Tidbits of the experience, at least. There was no way that man, so good-looking and sexy, had run his hands and mouth all over her and she hadn't remembered a whit of it.

Anyway, their union would be no more in about a half hour. It was fun to fantasize about what they might have done Saturday night, but only because it was just that—fantasy. And Reed would be out of her life very soon, just someone she'd say hi to in the coffee shop or grocery store. Maybe they'd even chuckle at the crazy time they'd up and gotten married by accident.

She waited for the doorbell to ring, but it didn't. Reed wouldn't be one to wait in the car and honk, so she peered out the window. He stood on the doorstep, typing something into his phone. Girlfriend, maybe. The man had to be involved with someone. He'd probably been explaining himself from the moment he'd left Norah's house this morning. Poor guy.

Her mom had already come to pick up the babies, so she was ready to go. She wore a casual cotton skirt and top for the occasion of getting back their marriage license, but in the back of her mind she was well aware she'd dolled up a little for the handsome cop. A little mascara, a slick of lip gloss, a tiny dab of subtle perfume behind her ears.

Which was all ridiculous, considering she was spending her morning undoing her ties to the man!

A text buzzed on her phone.

Not sure if the cutes are sleeping, so didn't want to ring the doorbell.

Huh. He hadn't been texting a girlfriend; he'd been texting *her*. Maybe there was no girlfriend.

She glanced at the text again. The warmth that spread across her heart, her midsection, made her smile. The cutes. An un-rung doorbell so as not to disturb the triplcts. If she needed more proof that Reed Barelli was top-notch, she'd gotten it.

She took a breath and opened the door. Why did he

have to be so good-looking? She could barely peel her eyes off him. "Morning," she said. "My mom has the triplets, so we're good to go."

"I got us coffee and muffins," he said, holding up a bag from Java Joe's. "Light, no sugar, right? That's how you took your coffee yesterday."

She smiled. "You don't miss much, I've been noticing."

"Plight of the detective. Once we see it, it's imprinted."

"What kind of muffins?" she asked, trying not to stare at his face.

"I took you for a cranberry-and-orange type," he said, opening the passenger door for her.

She smiled. "Sounds good." She slid inside his SUV. Clean as could be. Two coffees sat in the center console, one marked *R*, along with a smattering of change and some pens in one of the compartments.

"And I also got four other kinds of muffins in case you hate cranberry and orange," he said, handing her the cup that wasn't marked regular.

Of course he had, she thought, her heart pinging. She kept her eyes straight ahead as he rounded the hood and got inside. When he closed his door, she was ridiculously aware of how close he was.

"Thanks," she said, touched by his thoughtfulness.

"So, it's a half hour to the courthouse, we'll get back our license and that's that." He started the SUV and glanced at her.

She held his gaze for a moment before sipping her coffee to have something to do that didn't involve looking at him.

Would be nice to keep the fantasy going a little longer, she thought. *That we're married, a family, my mom is babysitting while we go off to the county seat to... admire the architecture, have brunch in a fancy place.* Once upon a time, this was all she'd wanted. To find her life's partner, to build a life with a great guy, have children, have a family. But everything had gotten turned on its head. Now she barely trusted herself, let alone anyone she wasn't related to.

Ha, maybe that was why she seemed to trust Reed. He was related to her. For the next half hour, anyway.

By the time they arrived at the courthouse, a beautiful white historic building, she'd finished her coffee and had half a cranberry-and-orange muffin and a few bites of the cinnamon chip. Reed was around to open her door for her before she could even reach for the handle. "Well, this is it—literally and figuratively."

"This is it," she repeated, glancing at him. He held her gaze for a moment and she knew he had to be thinking, *Thank God. We're finally here. Let's get this marriage license ripped up!*

They headed inside. The bronze mail slot on the side of the door loomed large. She could just imagine sneaky, old Abe Potterowski racing over and shoving all the licenses in. As they entered through the revolving door, Norah glanced at the area under the mail slot. Just an empty mail bucket was there.

Empty. Of course it was. Every step of this crazy process was going to be difficult.

After getting directions to the office that handled marriage licenses, they took the elevator to the third floor.

Maura Hotchner, County Clerk was imprinted on a plaque to the left of the doorway to Office 310. They went in and Norah smiled at the woman behind the desk.

"Ms. Hotchner, my name is Norah—"

"Good morning!" the woman said with a warm smile. "Ms. Hotchner began her maternity leave today. I'm Ellen Wheeler, temporary county clerk and Ms. Hotchner's assistant. How may I help you?"

Norah explained that she was looking for her marriage license and wanted it back before it could be processed.

"Oh dear," Ellen Wheeler said. "Being my first day and all taking over this job, I got here extra early and processed all the marriage licenses deposited into the mail slot over the weekend. Do you believe there were seventeen from Wedlock Creek alone? I've already put the official decrees for all those in the mail."

Norah's heart started racing. "Do you mean to tell me that my marriage to this man is legally binding?"

The county clerk looked from Norah to Reed, gave him a "my, you're a handsome one" smile, then looked back at Norah. "Yes, ma'am. It's on the books now. You're legally wed."

Oh God. Oh God. Oh God. This can't be happening.

She glanced at Reed, whose face had paled. "Can't you just erase everything and find our decree and rip it up? Can you just undo it all? I mean, you just processed it—what?—fifteen minutes ago, right? That's what the delete key is for!"

The woman seemed horrified by the suggestion. "Ma'am, I'm sorry, but I most certainly cannot just 'erase' what is legally binding. The paperwork has been processed. You're officially married."

Facepalm. "Is this the correct office to get annulment forms?" Norah asked. At least she wouldn't walk out of there empty-handed. She would get the ball rolling to undo this…crazy mistake.

Ellen's face went blank as she stared from Norah to Reed to their wedding rings and then back at Norah. "I have them right here."

Norah clutched the papers and hurried away. She could barely get to the bench by the elevators without collapsing.

Reed put his hand on her shoulder. "Are you all right? Can I get you some water?"

"I'm fine," she said. "No, I'll be fine. I just can't believe this. We're married!"

"So we are," he said, sitting beside her. "We'll fill out the annulment paperwork and I'm sure it won't take long to resolve this."

She glanced at the instruction form attached to the form. "Grounds for annulment include insanity. That's us, all right."

He laughed and held her gaze for a moment, then shoved his hands into his pockets and looked away.

"I guess I'll fill this out and then give it to you to sign?" she said, flipping through the few pages. She hated important forms with their tiny boxes. She let out a sigh.

He nodded and reached out his hand. "Come on. Let's go home."

For a split second she was back in her fantasy of him

being her husband and having an actual home to go to that wasn't falling down around her with sloping floors and a haunted refrigerator. She took his hand and never wanted to let go.

She really was insane. She had to be. What the hell was going on with her? It's like she had a wild crush on this man.

Her husband!

As Reed turned onto the road for Wedlock Creek, he could just make out the old black weather vane on top of his grandmother's barn in the distance. The house wasn't in view; it was a few miles out from here, but that weather vane, with its arrows and mother and baby buffalo, had always been a landmark when that old green car would get to this point for his stay at his grandmother's.

"See that weather vane?" he said, pointing.

Norah bent over a bit. "Oh yes, I do see it now."

"That's my grandmother's barn. When I was a kid heading up here from our house, I'd see that weather vane and all would be right in the world."

"I'd love to see the property," she said. "Can we stop?"

He'd driven over twice Saturday morning, right after he'd arrived in Wedlock Creek, but he'd stayed in the car. He loved the old ranch house and the land, and he'd keep it up, but it was never going to be his, so he hadn't wanted to rub the place in his own face. Though, technically, until his marriage was annulled, it *was* his. His grandmother must be mighty happy right now at his situation. He could see her thinking he'd finally settle down just to be able to have the ranch, then magically fall madly in love with his wife and be happy forever. Right.

He pulled onto the gravel road leading to the ranch and, as always, as the two-story, white farmhouse came into view, his heart lurched. Home.

God, he loved this place. For some of his childhood, when his grandfather had been alive, he'd stayed only a week, which was as long as the grouchy old coot could bear to have him around. But when he'd passed, his grandmother had him stay eight weeks, almost the whole summer. A bunch of times his grandmother had told his mother she and Reed could move in, but his mother had been proud and living with her former mother-in-law had never felt right.

Norah gasped. "What a beautiful house. I love these farmhouses. So much character. And that gorgeous red door and the black shutters…"

He watched her take in the red barn just to the left of the house, which was more like a garage than a place for horses or livestock. Then her gaze moved to the acreage, fields of pasture with shade trees and open land. A person could think out here, dream out here, *be* out here.

"I'd love to see inside," she said.

He supposed it was all right. He did have a key, after all. Always had. And he was married, so the property was out of its three-month limbo, since he'd fulfilled the terms of the will.

He led the way three steps up to the wide porch that wrapped around the side of the house. How many chocolate milks had he drunk, how many stories had his grandmother told him on this porch, on those two rocking chairs with the faded blue cushions?

The moment he stepped inside, a certain peace came over him. Home. Where he belonged. Where he wanted to be.

The opposite of how he'd felt about the small house he'd rented near the police department. Sterile. Meh. Then again, he'd had the place only two days and hadn't even slept there Saturday night. His furniture from his condo in Cheyenne fit awkwardly, nothing quite looking right no matter where he moved the sofa or the big-screen TV.

"Oh, Reed, this place is fantastic," Norah said, looking all around. She headed into the big living room with its huge stone fireplace, the wall of windows facing the fields and huge trees and woods beyond.

His grandmother had had classic taste, so even the furniture felt right to him. Brown leather sofas, club chairs, big Persian rugs. She'd liked to paint and her work was hung around the house, including ones of him as a boy and a teenager.

"You sure were a cute kid," Norah said, looking at the one of him as a nine-year-old. "And I'm surprised I never ran into you during your summers here. I would have had the biggest crush on that guy," she added, pointing at the watercolor of him at sixteen.

He smiled. "My grandmother didn't love town or people all that much. When I visited, she'd make a ton of food and we'd explore the woods and go fishing in the river just off her land."

The big, country kitchen with its white cabinets and

bay window with the breakfast nook was visible, so she walked inside and he followed. He could tell she loved the house and he couldn't contain his pride as he showed her the family room with the sliders out to a deck facing a big backyard, then the four bedrooms upstairs. The master suite was a bit feminine for his taste with its flowered rose quilt, but the bathroom was something—spa tub with jets, huge shower, the works. Over the years he'd updated the house as presents for his grandmother, happy to see her so delighted.

"I can see how much this place means to you," Norah said as they headed back downstairs into the living room. "Did it bother you that your grandmother wrote her will the way she did? That you had to marry to inherit it?"

"I didn't like it, but I understood what she was trying to do. On her deathbed, she told me she knew me better than I knew myself, that I did need a wife and children and this lone-wolf-cop nonsense wouldn't make me happy."

Maybe your heart will get broken again, but loss is part of life, Lydia Barelli had added. *You don't risk, you don't get.*

Broken again. Why had he ever told his grandmother that he'd tried and where had it gotten him? Those final days of his grandmother's life, he hadn't been in the mood to talk any more about the one woman he'd actually tried to be serious about. He'd been thinking about proposing, trying to force himself out of his old, negative feelings, when the woman he'd been seeing for almost a year told him she'd fallen for a rich lawyer—sorry. He hadn't let himself fall for anyone since, and that was over five years ago. Between that and what he'd witnessed about marriage growing up? Count him out.

Reed hadn't wanted to disappoint his beloved grandmother and had told her, "Who knows what the future holds?" He couldn't outright lie and say he was sure he'd change his mind about marriage. But he wouldn't let his grandmother go on thinking no one on this earth would ever love him. She wouldn't have been able to abide that.

"*Have* you been happy?" Norah asked, glancing at him, then away as if to give him some privacy.

He shrugged. "Happy enough. My work was my life and it sustained me a long time. But when I lost the only family I had, someone very special to me, I'll tell you, I *felt* it."

"It?" she repeated.

"Loss of…connection, I guess."

She nodded. "I felt that way when my dad died, and I had my mother, aunt and sister crying with me. I can't imagine how alone you must have felt."

He turned away, looking out the window. "Well, we should get going. I have to report to the department for my orientation at noon. Then it's full-time tomorrow."

"Thanks for showing me the house. I almost don't want to leave. It's so…welcoming."

He glanced around and breathed in the place. They had to leave. *He* had to leave. Because this house was never going to be his. And being there hurt like hell.

Chapter Five

Reed sat in his office in the Wedlock Creek Police Department, appreciating the fact that he had an office, even if it was small, with a window facing Main Street, so he could see the hustle and bustle of downtown. The two-mile-long street was full of shops and restaurants and businesses. The Pie Diner was just visible across the street if he craned his neck, which he found himself doing every now and again for a possible sighting of Norah.

His wife for the time being.

He hadn't seen her around today since dropping her off. But looking out the window had given him ideas for leads and follow-ups on a few of the open cases he'd inherited from his retired predecessor. Wedlock Creek might not have had a murder in over seventy years—

knock on wood—but there was the usual crime, ranging from the petty to the more serious. The most pressing involved a missing person's case that would be his focus. A thirty-year-old man, an ambulance-chasing attorney named David Dirk who was supposed to get married this coming Saturday, had gone missing three days ago. No one had heard from him and none of his credit cards had been used, yet there was no sign of foul play.

David Dirk. Thirty. Had to be the same guy. When Reed was a kid, a David Dirk was his nearest neighbor and they'd explore their land for hours during the summers Reed had spent at his grandmother's. David had been a smart, inquisitive kid who'd also had a father who'd taken off. He and Reed would talk about what jerks their dads were, then laud them as maybe away on secret government business, unable to tell their wives or children that they were really saving the world. That was how much both had needed to believe, as kids, that their fathers were good, that their fathers did love them, after all. David's family had moved and they'd lost touch as teenagers and then time had dissolved the old ties.

Reed glanced at the accompanying photo stapled to the left side of the physical file. He could see his old friend in the adult's face. The same intense blue eyes behind black-framed eyeglasses, the straight, light brown hair. Reed spent the next hour reading through the case file and notes about David's disappearance.

The man's fiancée, Eden Pearlman, an extensions specialist at Hair Palace on Main Street, was adamant that something terrible had happened to her "Davy Darling" or otherwise he would have contacted her. According to Eden, Davy must be lying gravely injured in a ditch somewhere or a disgruntled associate had hurt him, because marrying her was the highlight of his life. Reed sure hoped neither was the case. He would interview Ms. Pearlman tomorrow and get going on the investigation.

In the meantime, though, he called every clinic and hospital within two hours to check if there were any John Does brought in unconscious. Each one said no. Then Reed read through the notes about David's last case, which he'd won big for his client a few days prior to his disappearance. A real-estate deal that had turned ugly. Reed researched the disgruntled plaintiff, who'd apparently spent the entire day that David was last seen at a family reunion an hour away. Per the notes, the plaintiff was appealing and had stated he couldn't wait to see his opponent and his rat of a lawyer in court again, where he'd prevail this time. Getting rid of David in some nefarious way certainly wouldn't get rid of the case; Reed had his doubts the man had had anything to do with David's disappearance.

So where are you, David? What the heck happened to you?

Frustrated by the notes and his subsequent follow-up calls getting him nowhere, Reed packed up his files at six. Tomorrow would be his first full day on the force and he planned to find David Dirk by that day's end. Something wasn't sitting right in his gut about the case, but he couldn't put his finger on it. He'd need to talk to the fiancée and a few other people.

As he left the station, he noticed Norah coming out of a brick office building, wheeling the huge triple stroller.

He eyed the plaque on the door: Dr. Laurel McCray, Pediatrician. Brody in the front was screaming his head off. Bella was letting out shrieks. Or was that Bea? All he knew for sure was that one of the girls, seated in the middle, was quiet, picking up Cheerios from the narrow little tray in front of her and eating them.

He crossed the street and hurried up to her. "Norah? Everything okay?"

She looked as miserable as the two little ones. "I just came from their pediatrician's office. Brody was tugging at his ear all afternoon and crying. Full-out ear infection. He's had his first dose of antibiotics, but they haven't kicked in yet."

"Poor guy," Reed said, kneeling and running a finger along Brody's hot, tearstained cheek. Brody stopped crying for a moment, so Reed did it again. When he stood, Brody let out the wail of all wails.

"He really does like you," Norah said, looking a bit mystified for a moment before a mix of mom weariness came over her. "Even Bella has stopped crying, so double thank you."

As if on cue, Bella started shrieking again and, from the smell of things, Reed had a feeling she wasn't suffering from the same issue as her brother. People walking up and down the street stared, of course, giving concerned smiles but being nosey parkers.

Norah's shoulders slumped. "I'd better get them home."

"Need some help?" he asked. "Actually, I meant that rhetorically, so don't answer. You do need help and I'm going home with you."

"Reed, I can't keep taking advantage of how good you are with babies."

"Yes, you can. I mean, what are husbands for if not for helping around the house?"

She laughed. "I can't believe you actually made me laugh when I feel like crying."

"Husbands are good for that, too," he said before he could catch himself. He was kidding, trying to lighten her load, but he actually *was* her husband. And there was nothing funny about it.

"Well, you'll be off the hook in a few days," she said. "I filled out the annulment form and all you have to do is sign it and I'll send it in. It's on my coffee table."

She hadn't wasted any time. Or Norah Ingalls was just very efficient, despite having triplet babies to care for on her own. He nodded. "Well, then, I'm headed to the right place."

Within fifteen minutes they were in Norah's cramped, sloping little house. He held poor Brody while Norah changed Bella, who'd stopped shrieking, but all three babies were hungry and it was a bit past dinnertime.

Reed was in charge of Brody, who was unusually responsive to him, especially when his little ears were hurting, so he sat in front of Brody's high chair, feeding him his favorite baby food, cereal with pears. Norah was on a chair next to him, feeding both girls. Bella was in a much better mood now that her Cheerios had been replenished and she was having pureed sweet potatoes. Bea was dining on a jar of pureed green beans.

Reed got up to fill Brody's sippy cup with water when he stopped in his tracks.

On the refrigerator, half underneath a Mickey Mouse magnet, was a wedding invitation.

Reed stared at it, barely able to believe what he was seeing.

Join Us For
The Special Occasion of Our Wedding
Eden Pearlman and David Dirk...

Norah was invited to the wedding? He pulled the invitation off the fridge. "Bride or groom?" he asked, holding up the invitation.

Norah glanced up, spoon full of green bean mush midway to Bea's open mouth. "Groom, actually. I'm surprised he invited me. I dated David Dirk for two weeks a couple years ago. He ditched me for the woman he said was the love of his life. She must be, because I got that invitation about six weeks ago."

"You only dated for two weeks?" Reed asked.

She nodded. "We met at the Pie Diner. He kept coming in and ordering the pot pie of the day. I thought it was about the heavenly pot pies, but apparently it was me he liked. He asked me out. We had absolutely nothing in common and nothing much to talk about over coffee and dinner. But I'll tell ya, when my sister, Shelby, needed an attorney concerning something to do with her son Shane, I recommended David based on his reputation. He represented her in a complicated case and she told me he did a great job."

He tucked that information away. "No one has seen or heard from him in three days. According to the case notes, his fiancée thinks there was foul play, but my predecessor found no hint of that."

"Hmm. David was a real ambulance chaser. He had a few enemies. Twice someone said to me, 'How could you date that scum?'"

His eyebrow shot up. "Really? Recall who?"

"I'll write down their names for you. Gosh, I hope David's okay. I mean, he was a shark, but, like I said, when Shelby *needed* a shark, he did well by her. I didn't get to know him all that well, but he was always a gentleman, always a nice guy. We just had nothing much to say to each other. Zero chemistry."

He was about to put the invitation back on the fridge. "Mind if I keep this?" he asked.

She shook her head. "Go right ahead." She turned back to her jars of baby food and feeding the girls. "Brody seems calmer. The medicine must have kicked in." She leaned over and gave his cheek a gentle stroke. "Little better now, sweet pea?"

Brody banged on his tray and smiled.

"Does that mean you want some Cheerios?" Reed asked, sitting back down. He handed one to Brody, who took it and examined it, then popped it in his mouth, giving Reed a great gummy smile, three little jagged teeth making their way up.

Bea grabbed her spoon just as Norah was inching it toward her mouth and it ended up half in Bea's hair, half in Norah's.

"Oh, thanks," Norah said with a grin. "Just what I wanted in my hair." She tickled Bea's belly. "And now the three of you need a bath." She laughed and shook her head.

By eight o'clock, Norah had rinsed the baby food from her hair, all three babies had been fed, bathed, read to and it was time for bed. Reed stood by the door as Norah sang a lullaby in her lovely whispered voice. He almost nodded off himself.

"Well, they're asleep," she said, walking out of the nursery and keeping the door ajar. "I can't thank you enough for your help tonight, Reed."

"It was no trouble."

For a moment, as he looked into her hazel eyes, the scent of pears clinging to her shirt, he wanted to kiss her so badly that he almost leaned forward. He caught himself at the last second. What the hell? He couldn't kiss Norah. They weren't a couple. They weren't even dating.

Good Lord, they were married.

And he wanted to kiss her, passionately, kiss her over to that lumpy-looking gold couch and explore every inch of her pear-smelling body. But he couldn't, not with everything so weird between them. And things were definitely weird.

He was supposed to sign annulment papers. But those papers on the coffee table had been in his line of vision for the past two hours and he'd ignored them. Even after Norah had mentioned them when they'd first arrived tonight. "There are the papers," she'd said, gesturing with her chin. Quite casually.

But he'd bypassed the forms and fed Brody instead. Rocked the little guy in his arms while Norah gave his sisters a bath. Changed Brody into pajamas and sang his own little off-key lullaby about where the buffalos roamed.

And all he could think was *How can I walk away from this woman, these babies? How can I just leave them?*

He couldn't. Signing those annulment papers would mean the marriage never happened. They'd both walk away.

He didn't want to. Or he couldn't. One or the other. He might not want love or a real marriage, but that didn't mean he couldn't step up for Norah.

And then the thought he'd squelched all day came right up in Technicolor.

And if you stay married to Norah, if you step up for her, you can have your grandmother's ranch. You can live there. You can go home. You can all go home, far away from this crummy little falling-down house.

Huh. Maybe he and his new bride could make a deal. They could *stay* married. She'd feel safe every day.

And he could have the Barelli ranch fair and square.

She'd said she was done with romance, done with love. So was he.

He wondered what she'd think of the proposition. She might be offended and smack him. Or simply tell him the idea was ludicrous. Or she might say, "You know what, you've got yourself a deal" and shake on it. Instead of kiss. Because it would be an arrangement, not anything to do with romance or feelings.

He'd take these thoughts, this idea, back to the sterile rental and let it percolate. A man didn't propose a romance-less marriage without giving it intense consideration from all angles.

But only one thought pushed to the forefront of his head: that he wasn't walking away from Norah and the triplets. No way, no how. Like father, *not* like son.

* * *

Norah was working on a new recipe for a barbecue pot pie when the doorbell rang. Which meant it wasn't Reed. He'd just left ten minutes ago and wouldn't ring the bell knowing the triplets were asleep. Neither would her sister, mother or aunt.

Please don't be someone selling something, she thought as she headed to the front door.

Amy Ackerman, who lived at the far end of the street, stood at the door, holding a stack of files and looking exasperated. "Oh, thank God, you're here, Norah. I have to ask the biggest favor."

Norah tried to think of the last time someone had asked a favor of her. Early in her pregnancy, maybe. Before she started showing for sure. People weren't about to ask favors from a single mother of triplets.

"Louisa can't teach the zero-to-six-month multiples class and it starts Wednesday!" Amy shrieked, balancing her files in her hands. "Sixteen people have signed up for the class, including eight pregnant mothers expecting multiples. I can't let them down."

Amy was the director of the Wedlock Creek Community Services Center, which offered all kinds of classes and programming for children and adults. The multiples classes were very popular—the center offered classes in preparing for and raising multiples of all ages. How to feed three-week-old twins at once. How to change triplets' diapers when they were all soaked. How to survive the terrible twos with two the same age. Or three. Or four, in several cases.

During her pregnancy, Norah had taken the prep class and then the zero-to-six-month class twice herself.

At the time, she'd been so stressed out about what to expect that she'd barely retained anything she'd learned, but she remembered being comforted by just being there. She'd been the only one without a significant other or husband, too. She'd gotten quite a few looks of pity throughout and, during any partner activities, she'd had to pair up with the instructor, Louisa.

"Given that you just graduated from the real-life course now that the babes are seven months," Amy said, "will you teach it? You'll get the regular fee plus an emergency bonus. The class meets once a week for the next six weeks."

Norah stared at Amy, completely confused. "Me? Teach a class?"

"Yes, you. Who better? Not only do you have triplets, but you're a single mom. You're on your own. And every time I see you with those three little dumplings, I think, 'There goes a champ.'"

Huh. Norah, champ. She kind of liked it.

She also knew she was being buttered up big-time. But still, there was sincerity in Amy's eyes and the woman had always been kind to her. In fact, the first time Norah had signed up for the zero-to-six-month class, Amy had waived the course fee for her, and it wasn't cheap.

But how could she teach a class in anything? She was hardly a pro at being the mother of triplets. Last week Norah had made the rookie mistake of guiding her shopping cart in the grocery store a little too close to the shelves. Bella had managed to knock over an entire display of instant ramen noodles and either Bea or Brody had sent a glass jar of pickles crashing to the floor, blocking the path of a snooty woman who'd given Norah a "control your spawn" dirty look.

Then there was the time Norah had been waiting for a phone call from the pediatrician with test results, couldn't find her phone in her huge tote bag with its gobs of baby paraphernalia and had let go of the stroller for a second to dig in with both hands. The stroller had rolled away, Norah chasing after it. She'd caught someone shaking his head at her. Then there were all the times Norah had been told her babies should be wearing hats, shouldn't have pacifiers and "Excuse me, but are you really feeding your child nonorganic baby food? Do you know what's in that?"

Not to mention all the secret shame. How Brody had almost fallen off the changing table when she'd raced to stop Bea from picking up the plastic eye from a stuffed animal that had somehow come off in her crib. Norah could go on and on and on. She was no Super Mom of Multiples, ages zero to six months.

Thinking of all that deflated her, despite the fact that a minute ago, just being asked to teach the course had made her feel almost special, as though she had something to share with people who could use her help.

"Amy, I'm sorry, but I don't think—" Norah began.

Amy held up a hand. "If anyone is qualified to teach this class, it's you, Norah. And I promise you, I'm not just saying that because I'm desperate. Though I am desperate to find the right instructor. And that's you."

Norah frowned. "I make so many mistakes. All the time."

"Oh. You mean you're human? It's *not* easy taking care of baby triplets? Really?"

Norah found herself smiling. "Well, when you put it like that."

"There's no other way to put it."

"You know what, Amy? Sign me up. I will teach the class." Yeah, she would. Why not? She most certainly *had* been taking care of triplet babies—on her own—for seven months.

But she would have to hire a sitter or ask her mom or aunt to watch the triplets while she taught.

The fee for teaching was pretty good; paying a sitter every week would still leave a nice little chunk left over, and now she'd be able to afford to buy a wall-unit air conditioner for the downstairs. Norah had a feeling her mom and aunt would insist on watching the babies, though; both women had taken the class when Norah was in her ninth month. And even Shelby had signed up when she'd found herself the mother of not one but two six-month-old babies and needed to learn how to multitask on the quick.

The relief that washed over Amy's face made Norah smile. "You've saved me! Here's Louisa's syllabus and notes. You don't have to use her curriculum, though. You may have different ideas. It's your class now, so you make it your own."

That sounded good. "I'm looking forward to it," she said. "And thanks for asking me."

As Amy left, Norah carried the folder into the kitchen and set it down beside the bowl containing her special barbecue sauce, which wasn't quite there yet. Norah's regular barbecue sauce was pretty darn good, but she liked creating specials for the pot pies and wanted something with more of a Louisiana bite. She'd try a new batch, this time with a drop more cayenne pepper and a smidge less molasses. She'd just have to keep trying bits and dashes until she got it just right, which, now that she thought about it, was sometimes how parenting went. Yeah, there were basics to learn, but sometimes you had to be there, doing it, to know what to do.

As she headed to the coffeepot for a caffeine boost, she noticed the manila envelope on the counter. The annulment papers were inside. A yellow Post-it with Reed's name on the outside. Tomorrow she'd drop it off at the station and he'd sign them and she'd send them in or he would. And that would be the end of that.

No more Reed to the rescue, which had been very nice today.

No more fantasy husband and fantasy father.

No more sexy man in her kitchen and living room.

More than all that, she liked the way Reed made her feel. Despite his offers to help, he never looked at her as though she was falling apart or unable to handle all she had on her plate. He made her feel like she could simply use another hand...a partner.

Could the annulment papers accidentally fall behind the counter and disappear? She smiled. She liked this new and improved Norah. Kicking butt and teaching a class. Suddenly wanting her accidental husband to stick around.

Maybe because she knew he wouldn't?

Anyway, one out of two wasn't bad, though. At least she had the class.

Tomorrow she'd be out a husband.

Chapter Six

Norah had filled her tenth pulled pork pot pie of the morning when she noticed Reed Barelli pacing the sidewalk that faced the back windows of the Pie Diner's kitchen. He seemed to be deep in thought. She was dying to know about what. His missing person's case? Or maybe even…her? The annulment papers he'd forgotten to sign last night on his way out?

It's not like I reminded him, she thought. The way he'd come to her rescue last night like some Super Husband had brought back all those old fantasies and dreams. Of someone having her back. Someone to lean on, literally and figuratively. And, oh, how she would love to lean on that very long, sexy form of his, feel those muscular arms wrapped around her.

Focus on your work, she admonished herself. She

topped the pot pie with crust and made a design in the center, then set the pie on the tray awaiting the oven for the first of the lunch rush.

"Norah?" a waitress named Evie called out. "There's someone here to see you."

Had to be Reed. He was no longer out back. She quickly washed her hands and took off her apron, then left the kitchen. Reed sat at the far end of the counter. Since it was eleven, late for breakfast and early for lunch, the Pie Diner had very few customers. He was alone at the counter except for their regular, Old Sam, who sat at the first spot just about all day, paying for one slice of pie and coffee and getting endless refills and free pot pie for lunch, which had been the case for over a decade. Norah's mom had a soft spot for the elderly widower who reminded her of her late dad, apparently.

Reed looked…serious. Her heart sank. He must be there to sign the papers.

"I have the papers in my bag," she said. "Guess we both forgot last night. Follow me to the back office and you can sign them there if you want."

He glanced around, then stood and trailed her into the kitchen. The large office doubled as a kiddie nook and the triplets were napping in their baby swings.

She grabbed her tote bag from where it hung on the back of the desk chair and pulled out the annulment papers from the manila envelope.

But Reed wasn't taking the papers. He was looking at the babies.

"I'm glad they're here," he said. "Because I came to

say something kind of crazy and seeing the triplets reinforces that it's actually not crazy. That *I'm* not crazy."

She stared at him, no idea what he could be talking about.

He took the papers from her and set them down on the desk. "Instead of signing those, I have a proposition for you."

Norah tilted her head and caught her mother and aunt and sister all staring at them. She could close the door and give them some privacy, but then she'd only have to repeat what he'd said to her family, so they might as well get the earful straight from him. Besides, they'd never forgive her if she shut them out of this juicy part.

"A proposition?" she repeated.

Out of the corner of her eye, she could see her mother, sister and aunt all shuffle a step closer to the office.

He nodded. "If I sign those papers and you return them to the county clerk, poof, in a week, we're not married anymore. Never happened. Drunken mistake. Whoops. Except it *did* happen. And the intensive couple of days I've been a part of your life makes me unable to just walk away from you and Bella, Bea and Brody. I can't. A man doesn't do that, Norah."

Did she hear a gasp or two or three coming from the kitchen?

She stared at him. "Reed. We got married by accident. By drunken mistake, as you perfectly put it."

"Maybe so. But we also got married. We both stood up there and said our vows. Drunk off our tushes or not, Norah, we got married."

She gaped at him. "So you feel you have to stand by

vows you made under total insanity and drunken du-
ress? Why do you think both of those are grounds for
annulment?"

"I stand by you and the triplets. And if we're married,
if we stay married, I also get to have the Barelli ranch
fair and square. I was never planning on getting married. You said you weren't, either. We're both done with
love and all that nonsense about happily-ever-after. So
why not partner up, since we're already legally bound,
and get what we both need?"

"What do I need exactly?" she asked, narrowing her
eyes on him.

"You need a safe home, for one. A place big enough
for three children growing every single day. You need
financial stability and security. You need someone there
for you 24/7, having your back, helping, sharing the
enormous responsibility of raising triplets. That's what
you need."

No kidding. She did need that. She *wanted* that more
than she could bear to admit to herself. She also wanted
to take responsibility for her own life, her own children,
and do it on her own. And it was harder than she even
imagined it would be, than her mother had warned her
it would be when she'd been so set on moving out and
going it alone.

She couldn't be stubborn at the triplets' expense. She
would focus on that instead of on how crazy Reed's proposal was. Because when it came right down to it, he
was absolutely right about what she needed.

And what *he* needed was his grandmother's ranch.
She'd witnessed just how great that need was when

they'd been together at the house. The ranch meant so much to him. It was home. It was connection to his family. It was his future. And his being able to call the ranch home came down to her saying yes to his proposition.

Hmm. That proposition was a business deal of sorts. She thought, at least. "I get stability and security and you get the Barelli ranch."

He eyed her and she could tell he was trying to read her. She made sure she had on her most neutral expression. She had no idea what she thought of his proposal. Stay legally married to a man she'd known for days? For mutual benefit?

"Right," he said. "I need it more than I ever realized. It's home. The only place that's ever felt like home. You could move out of that falling-down, depressing little place and move to the ranch with room and wide-open spaces for everyone."

Her house *was* falling down and depressing. She hated those steep, slippery wooden stairs. And the lease was month to month. It would be a snap to get out of.

But the man was talking about serious legal stuff. Binding. He was talking about keeping their marriage on the books.

She looked up at him. "So we just rip up the papers and, voilà, we're married?"

"We are truly married, Norah. Yeah, we can go through with the annulment. Or we can strike a bargain that serves us both. Neither of us is interested in a real marriage about love and all that jazz. We've both been burned and we're on the same page. Our marriage would be a true partnership based on what we need. I think we'll be quite happy."

Quite happy? She wasn't so sure she'd be even close to happy. Comfortable, maybe. Not afraid, like she was almost all the time.

And what would it be like to feel the way she had during the ceremony? Safe. Secure. Cherished. Sure, the man "promising" those things had been drunk off his behind, but here he was, sober as a hurricane, promising those things all over again.

Maybe not to cherish her. But to stand at her side. God, she wanted that. Someone trustworthy at her side, having her back, being there.

But what did Reed Barelli, bachelor, know about living 24/7 with babies? What if she let herself say yes to this crazy idea, moved to that beautiful homestead and breathed for the first time in over seven months, and he couldn't handle life with triplets after a week? He had no idea what he was in for.

She raised an eyebrow. "What makes you think you want to live with three seven-month-old, teething babies? Are you nuts?"

He smiled. "Insane, remember?"

He had to be. She had to be. But what did she have to lose? If the partnership didn't work out, he would sign the papers and that would be that.

She could give this a whirl. After all, they were already married. She didn't have to do anything except move into a beautiful ranch house with floors that didn't creak or slope and with an oven that worked all the time.

Of course, she would be living with Reed Barelli. Man. Gorgeous man. What would *that* be like?

"Let's try," he whispered.

She looked up at him again, trying to read him. If she said, "Yes, let's try this wild idea of yours," he'd get his ranch. If she said no, he'd never have the only place that had ever felt like home. Reed wouldn't marry just to get the ranch; she truly believed that. But because of a big bowl of spiked punch, he had his one chance. He'd been so kind to her, so good to the triplets.

Brody let out a sigh and Norah glanced over at her son. His little bow-shaped mouth was quirking and a hand moved up along his cheek. The partnership would benefit the triplets and that was all she needed to know.

"I was about to say 'Where do I sign?' but I guess I'm not signing, after all." She picked up the papers and put them back in her tote bag.

The relief that crossed Reed's face didn't go unnoticed. Keeping that ranch meant everything to him. Even if it meant being awakened at 2:00 a.m. by one, two or three crying babies. And again at 3:00 a.m.

Out of the corner of her eye, Norah caught her mother hurrying back over to her station, pretending to be very busy whisking eggs. She poked her head out of the office. "Did y'all hear this crazy plan of his?"

"What? No, we weren't eavesdropping," her mother said. "Okay, we were. And I for one think his crazy plan isn't all that crazy."

"Me, too," Cheyenne said from in front of the oven. "You each get what you need."

Even if it's not what we really want, Norah thought.

Reed didn't want to be married. Just as she didn't. Sure, it felt good and safe. But even a good man like Reed couldn't be trusted with her stomped-on heart. No one could. It wasn't up for grabs, hadn't been since the day after she'd found out she was pregnant and had been kicked to the curb.

Shelby sidled over and took Norah's hand. "You don't mind if I borrow your wife, do you?" she asked Reed.

What also didn't go unnoticed? How Reed swallowed, uncomfortably, at the word *wife*.

Wife. Norah was someone's wife. Not just someone's—this man's. This handsome, kind, stand-up man.

"Of course," he said. "I'll keep an eye on the triplets."

Shelby gave him a quick smile, then led Norah by the hand to the opposite end of the kitchen. "Don't forget to figure out the rules."

"The rules?" Norah repeated.

"Just what kind of marriage will this be?" her sister asked. "He used the word *partnership*, but you're also husband and wife. So are you sharing a bedroom?"

Norah felt her face burn. She was hardly a prude, but the thought of having sex with Reed Barelli seemed... sinful in a very good way. They'd hardly worked up to the level of sex. Even if they were married. They weren't even at the first-kiss stage yet.

Norah pictured Reed in his black boxer briefs. "I guess we'll need to have a conversation about that."

"Yeah, you will," Shelby said. "Been there, done that with my own husband back when we first got together. Remember, Liam and I only got married so we could each have both our babies—the ones we'd raised for six months and the ones who were biologically ours."

Norah would never forget that time in Shelby's life. And the fact that all had turned out very well for her sister was a bonus. It wasn't as if Norah and Reed Barelli were going to fall in love. She had zero interest in romance. Yes, Reed was as hot as a man got, but nice to look at was different than feeling her heart flutter when she was around him. That wasn't going to happen. Not to a woman who'd been burned. Not to a busy mother of baby triplets. And it certainly wouldn't happen to Reed. He was even more closed to the concept of love and romance than she was. And as if he'd fall for a woman who'd lost all sex appeal. She smelled like strained apricots and spit-up and baby powder when she wasn't smelling like chicken pot pie. She wasn't exactly hot stuff these days.

"No matter what you're thinking, Norah, don't forget one thing," Shelby said.

Norah tilted her head. "What's that?"

Shelby leaned in and whispered, "He's a man."

"Meaning?"

"What's the statistic about how many times per second men think about sex?" Shelby asked.

Norah let out a snort-laugh and waved a hand down the length of herself. "Oh yeah, I am irresistible." She was half covered in flour. Her hair was up in a messy bun. She wore faded overalls and yellow Crocs.

"Trust me," Shelby said. "The issue will arise." She let out a snort herself. "Get it? *Arise*." She covered her mouth with her hand, a cackle still escaping.

"You're cracking jokes at a time like this?" Norah said, unable to help the smile.

"I'm just saying. You need to be prepared, Norah. Your life is about to change. And I'm not just talking about a change in address."

That was for sure. She'd be living with a man. Living with Reed Barelli. "Your words of wisdom?" she asked her sister.

"Let what happens happen. Don't fight it."

Norah narrowed her eyes. "What's gonna happen?"

"Let's see. Newlyweds move in together…"

Norah shook her head. "You can stop right there, sistah. We may be newlyweds, but like Reed said, this is a partnership. No hanky-panky. This isn't about romance or love. Nothing is *arising*."

"We'll see. But just know this, Norah. It's nice to be happy. Trust me on that."

Norah loved that her sister was happy. But the pursuit of happiness wasn't why Norah was saying yes to Reed's proposition.

"I'm finally at a good place, Shel," Norah said. "It took me a long time to bounce back from being abandoned the way I was. Lied to. Made a fool of. I might not be skipping all over town, but I'm not *un*happy. And I'm not throwing away my equilibrium when my first and foremost job is to be a good mother. I will not, under any circumstances, fall for a guy who's made it crystal clear he feels the same way I do—that love is for other people."

Shelby squeezed her hand. "Well, just know that anytime you need a sitter for an evening out with your husband, I'm available."

"I no longer need sitters because I'll have a live-in sitter."

"Answer for everything, don't you?" Shelby said with a nudge in Norah's midsection. She threw her arms around her and squeezed. "Everything's going to be fine. You'll see."

Norah went back into the office and stared hard at her sleeping babies, then at Reed, who leaned against the desk looking a bit…amused, was it?

"Your sister is right," he said. "Everything *is* going to be fine."

Norah wasn't so sure of that.

And had he heard *everything* they'd said?

Chapter Seven

Thanks to the Wedlock Creek PD going digital, copies of all the case files were now a click away and on Reed's smartphone. He was almost glad to have a confounding case to focus on for the next couple of hours while Norah packed for herself and the triplets.

For a while there he'd thought she might say no. The idea *was* crazy. To stay married? As a business partnership? Nuts. Who did that?

People like him whose wily grandmother had him over a barrel.

People like her who could use a solid place to land.

When he'd left the Pie Diner, the annulment papers back in the envelope, unsigned, the ranch rightfully his after a visit to his grandmother's attorney, an unfamiliar shot of joy burst inside him to the point he could have been drunk on spiked punch. The ranch was home for real. He'd wake up there every day. Walk the land he'd explored as a child and teenager. Finally adopt a dog or two or three and a couple of black cats that he'd always been partial to. He was going home.

But right now he was going to find David Dirk, who hadn't been seen or heard from in days. Reed sat in his SUV and read through the notes on his phone. Dirk's fiancée, Eden Pearlman, twenty-five, hair stylist, never before married, no skeletons in the closet, per his predecessor's notes, had agreed to meet with him at her condo at the far end of Main Street.

He stood in front of the building and took it in: five-story, brick, with a red canopy to the curb and a part-time doorman who had seen David Dirk leave for his office four days ago at 8:45 a.m., as usual, briefcase in one hand, travel mug of coffee in the other. He'd been wearing a charcoal-gray suit, red-striped tie. According to his predecessor's notes, David had had a full day's appointments, meetings with two clients, one prospective client, but had mostly taken care of paperwork and briefs. His part-time administrative assistant had worked until three that day and noted that David had seemed his usual revved-up self. Except then he vanished into thin air instead of returning home to the condo he shared with his fiancée of eight months.

Looking worried, sad and hopeful, Eden closed the door behind Reed and sat on a chair.

Reed sat across from her. "Can you tell me about the morning you last saw Mr. Dirk?"

Eden pushed her light blond hair behind her shoulders and took a breath. "It was just a regular morning. We woke up, had breakfast—I made him a bacon-and-cheese omelet and toast—and then David left for his office. He texted me a Thinking about you, beautiful at around eleven. That's the last time I heard from him. Which makes me think whatever went wrong happened soon after because he would have normally texted a cute little something a couple hours later and he didn't. He always texted a few times a day while at work. I just know something terrible happened! But I don't want that to be true!" She started crying, brown streaks under her eyes.

Reed reached for the box of tissues on the end table and handed it to her. She took it and dabbed at her eyes. "I know this isn't easy, Ms. Pearlman. I appreciate that you're talking to me. I'm going to do everything I can to find your fiancé. I knew David when I was a kid. We used to explore the woods together when I'd come up summers to stay with my grandmother. I have great memories of our friendship."

She sniffled and looked up at him. "So it's personal for you. That's good. You'll work hard to find my Davy Doo."

He wondered if any old girlfriend of his had ever referred to him as Reedy Roo or whatever. He hoped not. "What did you talk about over breakfast?" he asked.

"The wedding mostly. He was even trying to convince me to elope to Las Vegas—he said he wanted me to be his wife already and that we could even fly out that night. He's so romantic."

Hmm, making a case for eloping? Had Dirk wanted to get out of town fast? Was there a reason he'd wanted to go to Las Vegas in particular? Or was there a reason he'd wanted to marry Eden even faster than the weekend? "Did you want to elope?"

She shook her head. "My mother would have my head! Plus, all the invitations were out. The wedding is this Saturday!"

"Where?" he asked, trying to recall the venue on the invitation.

"The Wedlock Creek chapel—this Saturday night," she said, sniffling again. "What if he's not back by then?"

"I'm going to go out there and do my job," he said. "I'll be in touch as soon as I have news."

She stood and shook his hand. "Thanks, Detective. I feel better knowing an old friend of David's is on the case."

Back in his SUV, Reed checked David Dirk's financials again. None of his credit cards had been used in the past twenty-four hours. Reed's predecessor had talked to five potential enemies of David's from opposing cases, but none of the five had struck the retired detective as holding a grudge. Reed flipped a few more pages in the man's notes. Ah, there it was. "According to friends and family, however, David wouldn't have just walked out on Eden. He loved her very much."

So what did happen to you, David Dirk? Reed wondered.

Reed had sent a small moving truck with two brawny guys to bring anything Norah wanted from the house to the ranch, but since the little rental had come furnished, she didn't have much to move. Her sister had given her way too many housewarming gifts from her secondhand shop, Treasures, so Norah had packed up those items and her kitchen stuff and everything fit into a small corner of the moving truck. It was easier to focus on wrapping up her picture frames than on actually setting them on surfaces in Reed's home.

She was moving in with him? She was. She'd made a deal.

Norah had never lived with a man. She'd lived on her own very briefly in this little dump, just under a year, and while she liked having her own place and making her way, she'd missed hearing her mom in the kitchen or singing in the shower. Did Reed sing in the shower? Probably not. Or maybe he did. She knew so little about him.

She gave the living room a final sweep. This morning she'd done a thorough cleaning, even the baseboards because she'd been so wired, a bundle of nervous energy about what today and tomorrow and the future would be like. She was taking a big leap into the unknown.

"We're all set, miss," the big mover in the baseball cap said, and Norah snapped out of her thoughts.

She was about to transfer the triplets from their playpen to their car seats, then remembered her mom had them for the day to allow Norah a chance to settle in at Reed's. She stood in the doorway of her house, gave it a last once-over and then got in her car. She pulled out, the truck following her.

In fifteen minutes they were at the farmhouse. Reed told the movers to place all the items from the truck in the family room and that Norah would sort it all later.

Once the movers were gone and it was just Norah and Reed in the house, which suddenly seemed so big and quiet, it hit her all at once that this was now her home. She *lived* here.

"I want you to feel comfortable," he said. "So change anything you want."

"Did we talk about sleeping arrangements?" she asked, turning away and trying to focus on an oil painting of two pineapples. They hadn't, she knew that full well.

"I'll leave that to you," he said.

"As if there's more than one option?"

He smiled. "Why don't you take the master bedroom? It's so feminine, anyway." He started for the stairs. "Come, I'll give you more of a tour."

She followed him to the second level. The first door on the left was open to the big room with its cool white walls and huge Oriental rug and double wood dresser and big round mirror. A collection of old perfume dispensers was on a tray. A queen-size four-poster was near the windows overlooking the red barn, the cabbage-rose quilt and pillows looking very inviting. Norah could see herself falling asleep a bit easier in this cozy room. But still. "I feel like you should have the master suite. It's your house, Reed."

"I'd really rather have the room I had as a kid. It's big and has a great view of the weeping willow I used to read under. My grandmother kept it the same for when I'd come visit through the years. I'm nostalgic about it. So you take the master."

"Well, if you insist that I take the biggest room with

the en suite bath, who am I to say no?" She grinned and he grinned back. She walked inside the room and sat on the bed, giving it a test. "Baby-bear perfect. I'll take it." She flopped back and spread out her arms, giving in to this being home.

"Good, it's settled."

A vision of Reed Barelli in his black boxer briefs and nothing else floated into her mind again, the way he'd looked lying next to her, all hard planes and five-o'clock shadow, long, dark eyelashes against his cheeks. She had a crazy thought of the two of them in bed.

And crazy it was, because their marriage was platonic. Sexless.

Focus, Norah. Stop fantasizing, which is bad for your health, anyway. Men can't be trusted with any part of your anatomy. That little reminder got her sitting up. "My sister says we need to talk about how this is going to work."

"Your sister is right. I made a pot of coffee before you came. Let's go talk."

She followed him downstairs and into the kitchen. On the refrigerator was a magnet holding a list of emergency numbers, everything from 9-1-1 to poison control to the clinic and closest hospital. His work and cell numbers were also posted, which meant he'd put up this sheet for her.

He poured coffee and fixed hers the way she liked, set them both on the round table in front of the window and sat down. "I have a feeling we'll just have to deal with things as they come up."

She sat across from him, her attention caught by the

way the light shone on the side of his face, illuminating his dark hair. He was too handsome, his body too muscular and strong, his presence too…overwhelming.

"But I suppose the most important thing is that you feel comfortable here. This is now your home. Yours and the triplets. You and they have the run of the place. The crawl of the place."

She smiled. "I guess that'll take some getting used to." She glanced out the window at the fields she could imagine Bella, Bea and Brody running like the wind in just several months from now.

"No rush, right?" he said.

I could do this forever, she finished for him and realized that really was probably the case for him. He seemed to be at ease with the situation, suddenly living with a woman he'd accidentally slash drunk-married, appointing himself responsible for her and her three children. Because he wasn't attracted to her physically, most likely. Or emotionally. Men who weren't interested in marriage generally went for good-time girls who were equally not interested in commitment. Norah Ingalls was anything but a good-time girl. Unless you counted their wedding night. And you couldn't because neither of them could remember it.

Detective Reed Barelli's job was to serve and protect and that was what he was doing with his accidental wife. That was really what she had to remember here—and not let her daydreams get a hold on her. The woman he'd thought he was getting was Angelina, international flight attendant. Not Norah.

There was no need to bring up her sister Shelby's

bedroom questions again or exactly what kind of marriage this was. That was clear. They were platonic. Roommates. Sharing a home but not a bed. Helping each other out. Now that she had that square in her mind, she felt more comfortable. There were boundaries, which was always good. She could ogle her housemate, stare at his hotness, but she'd never touch, never kiss and never get her heart and trust broken again.

"Anything else we should cover?" he asked.

She bit her lip. "I think you're right. We'll deal with whatever comes up. Right now we don't know what those things might be."

"For instance, you might snore really loud and keep me awake all night and I'll have to remember to shut my door every night to block out the freight train sounds."

She smiled. "I don't snore."

"Not an issue, then," he said, and she realized that, again, he was trying to break the ice, make her feel more comfortable.

She picked up her mug. "You know who might keep you awake, though? The three teething seven-month-olds you invited to live here with you."

"They're supposed to do that, so it's all good."

"Does anything rattle you?" she asked, wondering if anything did.

"Yes, actually. A few things. The first being the fact that we're married. Legally married."

Before she could even think how to respond to that, he changed the subject.

"So what's your agenda for today?" he asked.

"I figure I'll spend the next couple of hours unpacking, then I'll be working this afternoon. It's Grandma's Pot Pie Day, so I'll be making about fifty classics—chicken, beef, vegetable—from my grandmother's recipes. Oh—and I'll be writing up a class syllabus, too."

He took a sip of his coffee and tilted his head. "A class syllabus?"

She explained about the director of the community services center asking her to teach the multiples class for parents and caregivers of zero-to-six-month-olds. "I tried to get out of it—I mean, I'm hardly an expert—but she begged."

"You *are* an expert. You're a month out of the age group. Been there, done that and lived to tell the tale. And to teach the newbies what to do."

She laughed. "I guess so!"

Norah always thought of herself as barely hanging on, a triplet's lovie falling out of the stroller, a trail of Cheerios behind them on the sidewalk, a runny nose, a wet diaper. Well-meaning folks often said, "I don't know how you do it," when they stopped Norah on the street to look at the triplets. Most of the time she didn't even feel like she *was* doing it. But all three babies were alive and well and healthy and happy, so she must be. She could do this and she would. She *did* have something to offer the newbie multiples moms of Wedlock Creek.

She sat a little straighter. She had graduated from the zero-to-six-month age range, hadn't she? And come through just fine. She was a veteran of those first scary six months. And yeah, you bet your bippy she'd done it alone. With help from her wonderful family, yes. But alone. She could teach that class blindfolded.

He covered her hand with his own for a moment and she felt the two-second casual touch down to her toes.

"Well, I'd better start unpacking," she said, feeling like a sixteen-year-old overwhelmed by her own feelings.

"If you need help, just say the word."

He was too good. Too kind. Too helpful. And too damned hot.

She slurped some more coffee, then stood and carried the mug into the family room, where the movers had put her boxes. But she wanted to be back in the kitchen, sitting with…her husband and just talking.

Her husband. She had a husband. For real. Well, sort of for real.

She didn't expect it to feel so good. She'd just had an "I'm doing all right on my own" moment. But it was nice to share the load. Really, really nice.

After walking Norah to the Pie Diner and taking a slice of Grandma's Classic Beef Pot Pie to go, Reed was glad the diner was so busy, because he kept seeing Norah's mom and aunt casting him glances, trying to sneak over to him for news and information about how Norah's move-in had gone. Luckily, they'd kept getting waylaid by customers wanting more iced tea and "could they have sausage instead of bacon in their quiche Lorraine?" and "were the gluten-free options really gluten free?"

Move-in had gone just fine. He was comfortable around Norah for some reason he couldn't figure out.

He'd never lived with a woman, despite a girlfriend or two dumping him over his refusal for even that, let alone an engagement ring.

As far as tonight went, he'd simply look at his new living arrangement the way he would with any roommate. They were sharing a home. Plain and simple. The snippets he'd overheard from Norah's conversation with her sister wouldn't apply. There would be no sex. No kissing. No romance. As long as he kept his mind off how pretty and sexy she was and remembered why they were staying married, he'd be fine.

That settled in his head, he hightailed it out of the Pie Diner with his to-go bag and took a seat at a picnic table edging the town green, waving at passersby, chatting with Helen Minnerman, who had a question about whether it was against the law for her neighbor's Chihuahua to bark for more than a minute when outside—no, it was not—and helping a kid around ten or eleven up from under his bike when he slid from taking a turn too fast.

Life in Wedlock Creek was like this. Reed could get used to this slower pace. A man could think out here in all this open space and fresh air, which was exactly what he was doing, he realized. Too much thinking. About his new wife and what it would be like to wake up every morning knowing she was in bed down the hall. In the shower, naked under a spray of steamy water and soap. Making waffles in his kitchen. Their kitchen. Caring for babies who had him wrapped around their tiny fingers after just a few days of knowing them.

But all his thinking hadn't gotten him closer to finding David Dirk. In fifteen minutes he was meeting Dirk's closest friend, a former law associate, so hopefully the man would be able to shed some light.

Reed finished the last bite of the amazing beef pot pie, then headed for Kyle Kirby's office in a small, brick office building next to the library.

Kirby, a tall, lanky man with black eyeglasses, stood when Reed entered, then gestured for him to sit. "Any luck finding David?"

Reed sat. "Not yet. And to be honest, not much is making sense. I've looked into all the possibilities and I'm at a loss."

Kirby was chewing the inside of his lip—as if he knew more than he wanted to say. He was looking everywhere but at Reed.

Reed stared at him. "Mr. Kirby, if you know where David is or if he's okay or not, tell me now."

Was that sweat forming on the guy's forehead despite the icy air-conditioning?

"I wish I could help. I really do." He stood. "Now, if those are all your questions, I need to get back to work."

Reed eyed him and stood. This was strange. Reed had done his homework on Kyle Kirby's relationship with David and the two were very close friends, had been since David had moved back to Wedlock Creek to settle down after graduating from law school. Kirby had no skeletons in his closet and there was no bad blood between him and David. So what was the guy hiding?

Frustrated, Reed put in a couple more hours at the station, working on another case—a break-in at the drugstore. A promising lead led to a suspect, and another hour later, Reed had the man in custody. The solid police work did nothing to help his mood over his inability to figure out what had happened to David. It was as if he had just vanished into thin air.

One staff meeting and the receptionist's birthday cake celebration later, Reed headed home. He almost drove to the house he'd rented and would need to find a new tenant for. It still hadn't sunk in that the Barelli ranch was his, was home, and that when he arrived, he wouldn't walk into an empty house. Norah would be there. Bella, Bea and Brody would be there. And tonight he was grateful for the company. Company that wouldn't be leaving. *That* would definitely take some getting used to.

He pulled up at the ranch, glad to see Norah's car. Inside he found her in the kitchen, the triplets in their big playpen near the window. Bella was chewing on a cloth book, Brody was banging on a soft toy piano and Bea was shaking a rattling puppy teether. The three looked quite happy and occupied.

"Something sure smells good," he said, coming up behind Norah and peeking into the big pot on the stove. "Pot pies for the diner?"

"Meatballs and spaghetti for us," she said. "I remember you mentioned you loved meatballs and spaghetti the night we met, so I figured it would be a good first dinner for us as—"

He smiled. "Official husband and wife."

"Official husband and wife," she repeated. She turned back to the pot, using a ladle to scoop out the meatballs and fragrant sauce into a big bowl. Was it Reed's imagination or did she look a little sad?

"You okay?" he asked.

She didn't answer. She picked up the pot of spaghetti and drained it into a colander over the sink, then added it to the bowl of meatballs and stirred it. Before he could say another word, the oven timer dinged and she took out heavenly smelling garlic bread.

"Well, can I at least help with anything?" he asked.

"Nope. The babies have eaten. Dinner is ready. The table is set. So let's eat."

She'd poured wine. There was ice water. A cloth napkin. He hadn't been treated to this kind of dinner at home in a long, long time, maybe not since he'd last visited his grandmother just weeks before she'd died.

"This is nice. I could get used to this," he said. "Thank you."

"You will get used to it because I love to cook and, given everything you're doing for me and the triplets, making dinner is the least I can do."

But as they chatted about their days and the triplets and she filled him in on some upcoming events in town, Norah seemed to get sadder. And sadder. Something was wrong.

"Norah. This marriage is meant to be a true partnership. So if something is bothering you, and something clearly is, tell me. Let's talk about it."

She poked at her piece of garlic bread. "It's silly."

"I'm sure it's not."

"It's just that, there I was, cooking at the stove in this beautiful country kitchen, my dream kitchen, the

triplets happily occupied in the playpen, and my husband comes home, except he's not really my husband
in the way I always thought it would go. I'm not com-
plaining, Reed. I'm just saying this is weird. I always
wanted something very different. Love, forever, growing old together on the porch. The works."

"It's not quite what I expected for myself, either," he
said, swirling a bite of spaghetti. "It'll take some getting used to. But we'll get to know each other and soon
enough we'll seem like any other old married couple."

"Kind of backward to have to get to know your
spouse." She gave him a wistful smile and took a sip
of wine.

"The triplets' father—you wanted to marry him?"

Norah put down her fork as though the mention of
him cost her her appetite. "I just don't understand how
someone could seem one way and truly be another way.
I got him so wrong. I thought he was crazy about me.
He was always talking about us and the future. But then
the future presented itself in the form of my pregnancy
and everything changed. I'll never forget the look on
his face when I told him I was pregnant. A combo of
freaked out and horrified."

"Sorry."

"And now everything I wanted—the loving husband,
the babies, a home for us—is right here and it's all…"

He touched her hand. "Not like the old dreams."

She lifted her chin and dug her fork into a meatball
with gusto. "I'm being ridiculous. I'm sitting here mop-
ing over what isn't and what wasn't. My life is my life.
Our deal is a good one. For both of us. And for those

three over there," she added, gesturing at the playpen. She focused on them for a moment and then turned back to him. "Okay, full speed ahead on the marriage partnership. My head is back in the game."

The meatball fell off her fork and plopped back onto her plate, sending a splatter of sauce onto both of them—her cheek and his arm. They both laughed and then he reached out and dabbed away the sauce from her cheek as she did the same to his arm.

"Anytime you need to talk this through, just tell me," he said. "And we'll work it out."

"You, too, you know."

He nodded. "Me, too."

As she pushed around spaghetti and twirled it but never quite ate any more, he realized she had the same funny pit in the middle of her stomach that he had in his, just maybe caused by a different emotion. She'd wanted something so much more—big passion, real romance, everlasting love—and had to settle for plain ole practical for a good reason. He'd planned on going it alone, never committing, but he had committed in a huge way, even if his heart wasn't involved. He was responsible for this family of four. Family of five now, including him.

He wouldn't let Norah down. Ever. But he knew he'd never be able to give her what she wanted in the deepest recesses of her heart.

Chapter Eight

There was no way Reed was getting any sleep tonight. Not with Norah down the hall, sleeping in who knew what. Maybe she slept naked, though he doubted she'd choose her birthday suit for her first night in her new home with her new partnership-husband. Twice he'd heard her get out of bed—the floor creaked a bit in that room—and go into the nursery. One of the babies had been fussing a bit and she sang a lullaby that almost had him drifting off. Almost. Norah had a beautiful voice.

He glanced at the clock: 2:12 a.m. He heard a faint cry. Then it grew louder. If he wasn't mistaken, that was Brody. He waited a heartbeat for the telltale creak of the master bedroom floor, but it didn't come. Only another cry did.

Reed got out of bed, making sure he was in more

than his underwear. Check. A T-shirt and sweats. He headed to the nursery and gently pushed the door open wider. One frustrated, red-faced little one was sitting up in his crib, one fist around the bar.

"Hey there, little guy," Reed said in his lowest voice to make sure he wouldn't wake Brody's sisters. "What's going on? What's with the racket?"

Brody scrunched up his face in fury that Reed wasn't picking him up fast enough. His mouth opened to let loose a wail, but Reed snatched him up and, as always, the sturdy little weight of him felt like pure joy in his arms. Brody wore light cotton footie pajamas and one sniff told Reed he was in the all clear for a middle-of-the-night, heavy-duty diaper change. He brought the baby over to the changing table and took off the wet diaper, gave Brody a sprinkle of cornstarch, then put on a new diaper like a pro. All the while, Brody looked at him with those huge slate-blue eyes.

Reed picked him up and held him against his chest, walking around the nursery while slightly rocking the little guy. Brody's eyes would flutter closed, then slowly open as if making sure Reed hadn't slipped him inside his crib and left. This went on four more times, so Reed sat in the rocker and Brody let out the sigh of all sighs and closed his eyes, his lips quirking and then settling.

"Guess that means you're comfortable, then," Reed whispered. He waited a few seconds, then stood, but the baby opened his eyes. Reed almost laughed. "Busted. You caught me." Reed sat back down, figuring he might be there awhile. Maybe all night. "Want to hear a story?"

Brody didn't make a peep in response, but Reed took that for a yes anyway.

"Once upon a time, there was a little boy named Beed Rabelli. That's not me, by the way."

Did Brody believe him? Probably not. But it made the story easier to tell.

"Well, this little kid, Beed, did everything to try to win his father's approval. His father's interest. But no matter what Beed did, pretending to be interested in things he really didn't even like, his father barely paid attention to him. He only came around every now and then as it was. But one day, Beed's dad never came around again and Beed started getting postcards from far-off places."

Brody moved his arm up higher by his ear and Reed smiled at how impossibly adorable the baby was. And what a good listener.

"So one day, Beed and his friend David Dirk were riding bikes and exploring the woods and they got to talking about how even though they pretty much had the same type of not-there dad, it didn't mean their dads didn't love them or care about them. Their dads were just…free spirits who had to follow the road in their souls. Or something like that. Anyway, Brody, I just want you to know that your father is like that and that's why he's not here. I don't want you to spend one minute wondering why he doesn't care about you, because I'm sure he does. He's just following that road that took him far away from here and—"

Reed stopped talking. Where the hell was this coming from? Why was he saying anything of this to Brody?

Because he cared about this little dude, that was why. And it was important to know because at some level it was very likely true.

He heard a sniffle and glanced toward Bea's and Bella's cribs. They were both fast asleep. He heard the sound again and realized it was coming from outside. Reed put Brody gently back inside his crib, and *booyah*—the baby did not open those eyes again. Either Reed had bored him to sleep or a story worked like it always had since time began.

He tiptoed out to investigate the sound of the sniffle. Was Norah so upset about her lost dreams that she was crying in the middle of the night?

He froze at the sight of her standing to the left of the nursery door, tears in her eyes.

"Norah? What's wrong?"

She grabbed him, her hands on the sides of his face, and pulled him close, laying one hell of a kiss on him. Damn, she smelled so good and her skin was so soft. Everything inside him was on fire. He backed her up against the wall and pressed against her, deepening the kiss, his hands roaming her neck, into her hair, down along her waist. He wanted to touch her everywhere.

"So you're not upset," he whispered against her ear, then trailed kisses along her beautiful neck.

"I was touched enough that you'd gotten up at a baby crying," she said. "And then as I was about to walk in, I heard you talking to Brody and couldn't help eavesdropping. I can't tell you how anxious I've been about the questions that would be coming my way someday, maybe at age three or four. 'Where's my father? Why doesn't Daddy live with us? Why doesn't Daddy ever see us? Doesn't he care about us?'"

Norah wiped under her eyes and leaned the front of her luscious body against Reed's. "I had no idea what I would say, how I could possibly make it okay for them. And one 2:00 a.m. diaper change later, you've settled it."

"Eh, I didn't say anything I hadn't worked out over the past twenty-nine years."

She smiled and touched his face, and he leaned his cheek against it. Then he moved in for another kiss, hoping reality and the night-light in the hallway wouldn't ruin the moment and make her run for her room.

She didn't. She kissed him back, her hands on his chest, around his neck, in his hair. He angled them down the hall toward his room and they fell backward onto his bed, the feel of her underneath him, every part of her against him, almost too much to bear.

He slid his hands under her T-shirt and pulled it over her head, then tugged off his own shirt and flung it behind him. He lay on top of her, kissing her neck, her shoulder, between her luscious breasts.

And then he felt her shift. Just slightly. The equivalent of a bitten lower lip. A hesitation.

He pulled back and looked at her. "Too fast?"

"Way too fast," she said. "Not that I'm not enjoying it. Not that I didn't start it."

He laughed. "That was hot. Trust me."

Her smile faded. "You've made it very clear what this marriage is, Reed. 'Friends with benefits' when we're married is too weird. Even for us. I think we need to keep some very clear boundaries."

She turned away from him and quickly put her T-shirt back on. He did the same.

"An emotional moment, the middle of the night, then there's me, still probably highly hormonal. Of course I jumped your bones."

She's trying to save face. Let her. "Believe me, if you hadn't kissed me, I would have kissed you first."

"Oh," she said, a bit of a smile back on her pretty face. "I guess we know whcrc we stand, then. We're foolishly attracted to each other on a purely physical level, and we went with the moment, then wised up. We'll just keep our hands to ourselves from now on. So that this partnership has a fighting chance."

She was right. If they screwed this up with great sex, that could lead to who knew what, like other expectations, and suddenly she would be throwing annulment papers at him, all his plans to stand by her and the triplets would fall to pot. And so would this ranch—home.

He nodded. Twice to convince himself of just how right she was. "We both know where romance leads. Trouble. Heartache. Ruin."

"Well, at least the mystery is gone. You've seen my boobs."

He had to laugh. But he sobered up real fast when he realized the mystery was hardly gone. He had yet to truly touch her.

"So if I let what happens happen and then we realize it's a bad idea, what does that mean?" Norah asked Shelby the next morning as they sat at a corner table for two in Coffee Talk, their favorite place to catch up in Wedlock Creek. Their huge strollers against the wall behind them, triplets asleep and Shelby's toddler sons drifting off after a morning running around the playground, the sisters shared a huge slice of delicious crumbly coffee cake. Of course they'd never have pie anywhere but at their own family restaurant.

"Ooh, so something happened?" Shelby asked, sipping her iced mocha.

"In the middle of the night last night, I thought I heard one of the babies crying, but when I went to the nursery, Reed was sitting in the rocker with Brody in his arms, telling him a story about himself and relating it to Brody. I stood there in tears, Shel. This is going to sound crazy, but in that moment, my heart cracked open."

Shelby's mouth dropped open. "You're falling in love!"

"Oh God, I think I am. I was so touched and so hormonal that I threw myself at him. But then I realized what an idiot I was being and put the kibosh on that."

"What? Why?"

"Shelby, he's made it crystal clear he married me for his ranch. And because he feels some kind of chivalrous duty toward me, as if annulling our marriage means he's walking away from his responsibilities. He's not responsible for us!"

"He feels he is," Shelby said. "The man's a police officer. Serve and protect. It's what he does."

Maybe that was a good reminder that Reed was operating on a different level—the cop level, the responsibility level. His father had walked away from him and his mother, the triplets' father had walked away from them and Norah, and Reed couldn't abide that, couldn't stand it. So he was stepping in. Attracted to her physically or not, Reed's feelings where she was concerned weren't of the romantic variety. He was trying to right wrongs.

"Um, excuse me?" a woman asked as she approached the table.

"Hi," Norah said. "Can we help you?"

"I noticed your triplets," she said, looking at Bella, Bea and Brody, who were all conked out in their stroller wedged up against the wall. "So it's true? If you get married at the Wedlock Creek chapel, you'll have multiples?"

"I didn't get married at the chapel and still had triplets," Norah said.

"And I did get married at the chapel and had one baby," Shelby said, "but ended up with twins, sort of." At the woman's puzzled expression, she added, "It's a long story."

Norah took a sip of her iced coffee. "Well, the legend does say if you marry at the chapel you'll have multiples in some way, shape or form. Are you hoping for a houseful of babies all at the same time?" she asked the woman.

"My fiancé is a twin and so we have a good chance of having twins ourselves, but he wants to increase our luck. I just figure the legend is just that—a silly rumor."

"No way," Shelby said. "Last year alone, there were five multiple births—two sets of triplets and three twins. The year before, four sets of twins and one set of triplets. The year before that, one set of quadruplets and two sets of twins. And that's just in Wedlock Creek."

The woman paled. She truly seemed to lose color. "Oh. So the legend is actually true?"

"Well, as true as a legend can be," Shelby said. "But

this town is full of multiples. We can both personally attest to that."

"Um, is that a bad thing?" Norah asked gently.

"Well, twins just seem like a lot," the woman said. "One seems like a lot. I want to be a mother, but two at once? I don't know. I don't think I want to help our chances, you know?"

Norah smiled. "Then you definitely don't want to marry at the Wedlock Creek chapel." She upped her chin out the window. "See that woman? Pregnant with triplets. All boys!"

The woman swallowed. "I think we'll marry at the Brewer Hotel. Thanks!" she said and practically ran out.

Shelby laughed. "One baby *is* a lot of work. She's not wrong."

"But the more the merrier," Norah said, lifting her iced coffee for a toast.

"Got that right," Shelby said and tapped her cup. "Of course, you know what this means."

"What what means?"

"You and Reed got married at the chapel. You're going to have more multiples. Omigod, Norah, you're going to have, like, ten children."

She imagined three babies that looked like Reed Barelli. The thought made her smile.

"Jeez, you are far gone," Shelby said.

"Heaven help me. But I am."

She was falling in love with her business partner of a husband. She had to put the brakes on her feelings. But how did you do that when the floodgates just opened again?

Chapter Nine

That night, Norah arrived at the Wedlock Creek Community Services Center with her stack of handouts, her laptop, for her slideshow on her favorite baby products, and a case of the jitters. As she stood at the front of the room, greeting students as they entered, she took a fortifying gulp of the coffee she'd brought in a thermos. As she'd left the ranch, she was surprised by how much she wished Reed had been there to see her off and give her a "you've got this" fist bump or something. She was beginning to need him a little too much for comfort. But he was working late, following up on a promising lead about David Dirk, who was still missing.

A woman's belly entered the room before she did. "If my water breaks while I'm sitting down, here's my husband's cell number," she said to Norah with a smile. "I'm not due for another month, but you never know."

You never know. No truer words ever spoken.

Norah smiled and took the card with the woman's husband's information. "I'm glad you're here. And if your water does break, I've got my cell phone at the ready and a list of emergency medical numbers."

"Pray I don't give birth until after the last class!" the woman said on a laugh. "I need to learn everything!" she added and slowly made her way over to the padded, backed benches that had been brought in specifically for women in her condition.

There were several pregnant women with their husbands, mothers, mothers-in-law and various other relatives all wanting to learn the basics of caring for newborn multiples. Several women had infant multiples already. Norah glanced around the room, seeing excitement and nerves on the faces. That was exactly how she'd felt when she'd shown up for the first class.

She was about to welcome her students when the door opened and Reed walked in. "Sorry I'm a minute late," he said, handing her a printout of his online registration form. He took an empty seat next to one of the husbands, giving the man a friendly nod.

Reed was taking her class?

Of course he was.

Norah smiled at him and the smile he gave her back almost undid her. *Don't think about what happened in the hallway last night*, she ordered herself. *Stop thinking about his hands on your bare skin. You're standing in front of a room full of people!*

She sucked in a breath, turned her attention away

from Reed and welcomed her students. "Eight months ago, I was all of you," she said. "I was nine months' pregnant with BGG triplets—that's boy, girl, girl—and I was a nervous wreck. Not only was I about to give birth to three helpless infants who would depend on me for everything, but I was a single mother. I will tell you right now that the most important thing I have learned about being the mother of triplets, particularly in my position, is to ask for help."

Norah looked around the room. All eyes were on her, interested, hanging on her every word, and some were actually taking notes.

So far, so good, she thought. "Ladies, don't expect your husbands to read your minds—if you want him to change Ethan while you change Emelia, ask him! No passive-aggressive stewing at the changing table while he's watching a baseball game. Speak up. Ask for what you need!"

"She's talking to you, Abby," the man next to Reed said and got a playful sock in the arm from his wife.

The students laughed. This was actually going well! She was standing there giving advice. People were responding! "And men, while you have infant twins or triplets or quadruplets, you're not going to be watching the game unless you have a baby or two propped in your arms, one hand on a bottle, the other burping another's little back."

A guy got up and headed for the door. "Just kidding," he said with a grin. More laughter.

Norah smiled. "And you grandmothers-to-be...what I learned from my mother? You're the rock. You're going to be everything to the mother and father of newborn multiples. Not only do you have experience, even if it's not with multiples yourselves, but you've been there, done that in the parenting department. You love those little multiples and you're there to help. Sometimes your brand-new mother of a daughter or daughter-in-law may screech at you that she's doing it her way. Let her. Maybe it'll work, maybe it won't. But what matters is that you're supporting one another. You're there."

She thought of her mother and her aunt Cheyenne and her sister. Her rocks. She couldn't have done it without them—their love and support and good cheer.

"So that's my number one most valuable piece of information I can offer you. Ask for help when you need it. When you think you'll need it. Because you will need it. If some of you don't have a built-in support system, perhaps you can create one when you go home tonight. Friends. Caring neighbors. Folks from your house of worship. Think about the people you can turn to."

From there, Norah started up her slideshow of products she'd found indispensable. She talked about cribs and bassinets. Feeding schedules and sleep schedules. How laundry would take over entire evenings.

"You did all that on your own?" a woman asked.

"I lived on my own, but I have a fabulous mother, fabulous aunt and fabulous sister who were constantly over, taking shifts to helping me out, particularly that first crazy month. So when I tell you help is everything, I mean it. Just don't forget that thank-yous, hugs and homemade pies go a long way in showing appreciation for their support."

Fifty-five minutes later the class was winding down. Norah let them know that in two weeks she'd be bringing in her triplets for show-and-tell with her mom as a volunteer assistant, demonstrating how to perform necessary tasks with three babies. After a question-and-answer session, Norah dismissed the students.

Huh. She'd really done it. She'd taught a class! And she was pretty darn good at it.

One of the last to pack her notebook and get up was a woman who'd come to the class alone. Early thirties with strawberry blond hair, she looked tired and defeated and hadn't spoken much during the period. She walked up to Norah with tears in her eyes.

Oh no. This woman had the look of multiple-itis.

"I have twin six-week-olds," the woman said. "My mother is with them now, thank God. They're colicky and I'm going to lose my mind. My husband and I argue all the time. And I only have twins—the bare minimum to even have multiples—and I'm a falling-apart wreck!"

Norah put her hand on the woman's arm. "I totally hear you." She offered the woman a commiserating smile. "What's your name?"

"Sara Dirk."

Norah noticed Reed's eyebrows shoot up at the name Dirk.

"Welcome, Sara. I'm really glad you're here. I haven't personally dealt with colic, but I've known colicky babies, and let me tell you, you might as well have sextuplets."

Sara finally smiled. "They don't stop crying. Except to breathe. I don't know how my mother does it—the screeching doesn't even seem to bother her. She just walks up and down with one baby while she watches the other in the vibrating baby swing, then switches them. I hear those cries that go on forever and I just want to run away."

Reed walked over and sat in the chair at the side of the desk, collecting Norah's handouts. She knew he was intently listening.

"That's wonderful that your mom is so supportive, Sara. I tell you what. Stop by the Pie Diner tomorrow and let anyone there know that Norah said they're to give you two of your and your mom's favorite kinds of pies on the house."

"I love the Pie Diner's chocolate peanut butter pie. It always cheers me up for a good ten minutes."

Norah smiled. "Me, too. And I'll research some tips for dealing with colic," she said. "I'm sure you have already, but I'll talk to the mothers I know who've dealt with it and survived. I'll email you the links."

"Thanks," she said. "I really appreciate it."

Reed stood with Norah's folders and laptop. He extended his hand to Sara. "Did I hear you say your last name is Dirk?"

Sara nodded.

"Are you related to David Dirk?" he asked.

Sara nodded. "My husband's first cousin."

"I'm Reed Barelli, a detective with the Wedlock Creek Police Department. I also knew David when I was a kid. I'm trying to find him."

"I sure hope he's okay," Sara said. "We just can't figure out what could have happened. The night before he went missing, he stopped by for a few minutes to drop off a drill he'd borrowed from my husband and he seemed so happy."

"Any particular reason why—besides the upcoming wedding, I mean?" Reed asked.

"He said something had been bothering him but that he'd figured out a solution. And then the twins started screaming their heads off, as usual, and there went the conversation. He left and that was the last time I saw him."

"Do you know what was bothering him?" Reed asked.

"No idea. I know he's madly in love with Eden. Things are going well at work, as far as I know."

"When did you see him before that last time?" Reed asked.

"Hmm, maybe a couple nights before. We—my husband and I—needed a sitter for an hour and my mother couldn't do it, so we begged David. He and Eden watched the twins. Do you believe that after babysitting our little screechers, that woman is hoping for triplets or even quadruplets? Craziest thing. She loves the idea."

"More power to her," Norah said.

"Well, I'd better get back and give my mother a break. See you next week, Norah. Oh, and, Detective Barelli, I do hope you find David. Eden must be out of her mind with worry."

Norah watched Reed wait until Sara had left, then hurried to the door and closed it.

"Are you thinking what I'm thinking?" he asked.

"I have so many thoughts running through my head that it could be any number of them."

"About David Dirk. And why he suddenly went missing."

Norah tilted her head and stared at Reed. "What do you mean?"

"Well, let's recount the facts and evidence. David

Dirk has a cousin with colicky twins. David Dirk and his fiancée babysit said colicky twins. Despite the screeching in their ears for over an hour, Eden is hoping for multiples."

Norah wasn't sure where he was going with this. "Okay," she said. "What does that have to do with his disappearance?"

"Well," he continued, "she and David are to be married at the Wedlock Creek chapel, where legend says those who marry will be blessed with multiples. The night before he went missing, David told Sara something was bothering him but he'd figured out a solution. Cut to David's fiancée telling me that on the morning he disappeared, he'd asked her to elope. But she reminded him how badly she wanted to marry at the chapel."

Ah. Now she was getting it. "Oh boy."

"Exactly. Because why would David want to elope instead of marrying at the Wedlock Creek chapel?

"The only reason folks in this town don't get married there is because they don't want multiples." But was David really so freaked out by his cousin's colicky babies and his fiancée wanting sextuplets that he ran away? No way. Who would do that? She herself had dated him, and he'd seemed like a stand-up guy, even if they'd had zero to talk about other than the weather and which restaurants they liked in town.

She remembered the woman who'd approached her and Shelby in the coffee shop yesterday. She'd wanted to avoid that legend like the ole plague. So maybe it was true. David had run!

"I'm thinking so," Reed said. "It's the only thing that makes sense. Yesterday I spoke with a friend of his who seemed nervous, like he was hiding something. Maybe he knew the truth—that David took off on his own—and had been sworn to secrecy."

"What a baby David is," Norah said.

"Pun intended?"

Norah laughed. "Nope. He's just really a baby. Why not tell Eden how he felt? He has family and friends scared that something terrible happened to him. He had a friend lie to a police officer."

"Based on everything I've heard, I'm ninety-nine percent sure he took off on his own. I just have to find him. Maybe the friend can shed some light. I doubt he'll tell me anything, though."

"So how will you find David, then?"

"The right questions," Reed said. "And maybe my own memories of where David would go when his world felt like it was crashing down. I might know where he is without even realizing it. I need to do some thinking."

She nodded. "So let's go home, then."

"Home to the ranch. I like the sound of that."

Norah smiled and took his hand before she realized they weren't a couple. Why did being a couple feel so natural, then?

"Tell me more about the legend of the Wedlock Creek chapel," Reed said to Norah as they sat in the living room with two craft beers and two slices of the Pie Diner's special fruit pie of the day—Berry Bonanza.

"Well, as far as I know, back in the late 1800s, a woman named Elizabeth Eckard, known for being a bit peculiar, married her true love at the chapel."

"Peculiar how?"

"Some say she was a witch and could cast spells," Norah explained. "It was just rumor, but most shunned her just in case they got on her bad side."

Reed raised an eyebrow. "Apparently her true love wasn't worried."

Norah smiled. "Legend says he was so in love with Elizabeth, he married her against his parents' wishes, who refused to have anything to do with them."

"Jeez. Harsh."

"Yup. But he loved her and so he married her at the beautiful chapel that she had commissioned to be built. Elizabeth had inherited a bit of money and wanted the new town of Wedlock Creek to have a stately chapel for services of all kinds."

Reed took a bite of the pie. "That must have buttered up the townspeople. Did his family come around?"

"Nope. And the townspeople still shunned her. Some even avoided services at the chapel. But some started noticing that those who attended church seemed luckier than those who didn't. And so everyone started going."

Reed shook his head. "Of course."

"Well, the luck didn't extend to Elizabeth. All she wanted was children—six. Three boys and three girls. But she never did get pregnant. After five years of trying, her husband told her there was no point being married to her if she couldn't give him a family, and he left her."

"That's a terrible story," Reed said, sipping his beer.

Norah nodded. "But Elizabeth loved children and ended up turning her small house into a home for orphans. She had the children she'd always wanted so much, after all. But when her only sister found herself in the same position, not getting pregnant, her sister's husband went to the officiants of the chapel and demanded an annulment. That night, Elizabeth crept out to the chapel at midnight and cast a spell that those who married at the chapel would not only be blessed with children, but multiples."

"Come on," Reed said.

Norah shrugged. "Nine months later, Elizabeth's sister had twin girls. And all the couples who married at the church that year also had multiples. Whispers began that Elizabeth had blessed the church with a baby spell."

"Did she ever marry again? Have her own multiples?"

Norah shook her head. "No, but she took in orphans till her dying day, then hired people to keep the home going. It was going strong until the 1960s, when foster care became more prominent."

"It's crazy that I actually think that David Dirk, reasonable, intelligent, suspicious of everything, believes in this legend to the point that he fled town to avoid marrying at the chapel. It's just an old legend. There's no blessing or spell."

"Then what accounts for all the multiples?" Norah asked.

"A little help from science?" he asked.

"Maybe sometimes," she said. "But I know at least ten women who married at the chapel and had multiples without the help of a fertility doctor."

"Don't forget me," he said.

"You?"

"I married at the chapel and now I have triplets."

She smiled, but the beautiful smile faded. "Are you their father, Reed? I mean, we didn't actually ever talk about that. You said you felt responsible for them and me. You said you would help raise them and help support them and be there for them. But are you saying you want to be their father?"

He flinched and realized she caught it. "I—" He grabbed his beer and took a swig, unsure how to answer. *Did* he want to be the triplets' father? He was their mother's husband—definitely. He was doing all the things Norah said when it came to caring for Bella, Bea and Brody. He was there for them. But was he their *father*?

That word was loaded.

"This is a partnership," she said, her voice formal as she sat straighter. "Of course you're not their *father*." She waved a hand in the air and made a strange snorting noise, then cut a forkful of berry pie. "It was silly of me to even use the term." A forced smile was plastered on her face. "So where do you think David Dirk is?"

Should he let her change the subject? If he were half the person she thought he was, he wouldn't. They'd talk this out. But he had no idea how he felt about this. Their *father*? Was he anyone's father? Could he be? Did he *want* to be?

"Norah, all I know for sure is that I want to take care of the four of you. I'm responsible for you all."

Her lips were tightly pressed. "Because you drunk-married me."

"I'm legally wed to you. It might have been because of spiked punch, but being married serves us both."

"You got your ranch," she said, staring at him. "And I got some security. I just have to keep reminding myself of that. Why we're here. Why we did this. Crazy as it really is."

Was it all that crazy? No. They both got what they needed.

He wasn't anyone's father. Reed Barelli? A father? With his craptastic model of paternity?

"It's good to know, to remember, what we are," she said, her voice higher pitched.

Higher pitched because she was upset? Or because she was stating a fact? They'd almost had sex, but she'd called a halt and wisely so. She knew messing around with their partnership could have terrible consequences. Anything that could put conflict between them could ruin a good thing. And this marriage was a good thing. For both of them.

He was no one's father. He was Norah's husband and caretaker of her children. Guardian of them all.

None of this sounded right. Or felt right. His shoulders slumped and he slugged down the rest of the beer.

"Maybe I should go pick up the babies," she said. "My mom wants to keep them overnight, but I'm sure she'd rather have a solid night's sleep."

She wanted—needed—a buffer, he realized. And so did he.

"I'll go with you," he said. "Tell you the truth, I miss their little faces."

She bit her lip and lifted her chin, and he also realized he'd better stop saying things like that, despite the fact that it was the truth. His affection for the triplets was also a good thing—the fact that they had his heart meant he'd be a good provider, a good protector.

And that was what he'd vowed to be.

Chapter Ten

The next morning, Norah woke very early and made twelve pot pies to deliver to the Pie Diner, the need to keep her eyes and mind on the various pots and timers a help in keeping her mind off Reed. But as she slid the last three pies from the oven, the smell of vegetable pot pie so comforting and tantalizing that she took out a frozen one to heat up for her breakfast, she couldn't stop hearing him say he wasn't the triplets' father.

She knew that. And of course, he didn't say it outright because he was Reed Barelli. But she'd been under the impression that fatherhood was part of the deal. Until she'd heard what had come stumbling out of her own mouth last night. He'd said again that being married, spiked punch or not, served them both. And she'd said something like, "Right, you got your ranch, I got some security."

Security. That was very different than "a father for my children."

Her shoulders slumped. Maybe she hadn't thought this through quite far enough. A father for her kids should have been first on her list, no?

Except you weren't looking for a father for your kids, dummy, she reminded herself. *You weren't looking for anyone. You got yourself in a situation and you didn't undo it so that you and your babies could have that security: a safe house, another caring adult, the financial burden lifted a bit, one more pair of hands. All that in a kind, supportive—and yes, sexy as all get-out—husband.*

No one, certainly not Reed Barelli, had used the word *father.*

Okay. She just had to let it sink in and accept it. Her marriage was platonic. Her husband was not her children's father. She had a good setup. It was good for the both of them.

"Do people eat pot pie for breakfast?" Reed asked as he walked into the kitchen in a T-shirt and navy sweats. Even his bare feet were sexy. His hair was adorably rumpled and as the sunlight illuminated half his face, he looked so beautiful she just stood there and stared at him until he tilted his head.

"Pot pie is appropriate for all meals," she said. "Seven a.m. Three p.m. Six p.m."

"Good, because this kitchen smells so good I'm now craving it."

"You're in luck because I have six frozen in the freezer. Just pop one in the oven for a half hour. It'll be ready when you're out of the shower." She glanced at her watch. "I'm going to drop these off at the Pie Diner and pick up the babies, bring them home and then go to Sara Dirk's with some frozen pot pies. I think she could use a freezer full of easily reheatable meals."

"That's thoughtful of you. Tell you what. Why don't you go to Sara's and I'll deliver the pies and pick up the rug rats and bring them home. I'm not on duty till noon."

"I can pick up the triplets," she said, her stomach twisting. "They're my children and I—"

"Norah," he said, stepping closer. He took both her hands and held them. "That's why I'm here. That's why you're here. I'm now equally responsible for them. So go."

He sure did use the word *responsible* a lot. She had to keep that in mind. *Responsible* was how he'd gotten himself married to her in the first place. He'd heard the plaintive, wistful note in her voice—*I've always dreamed of getting married here*—and instead of running for the hills, he'd felt responsible for her lost dreams and picked her up in his arms and carried her inside the chapel and vowed to love, honor and cherish her for the rest of his days.

She glanced down at their entwined hands. Why did it have to feel so good? Why did she have to yearn for more than the deal they'd struck? "Thank you, then," she managed to say, moving to the freezer to pull out six pot pies for Sara. The icy blast felt good on her hot, Reed-held hands and brought her back to herself a bit. "I'll pop one in the oven for you. Thirty minutes, okay?"

"Got it. See you back at home in a bit."

Back at home. Back at home. As she carried her bag

to the door, she looked around and realized this ranch didn't feel like home, that she wasn't quite letting herself feel that it was hers, too. It wasn't. Not really. Just like Reed wasn't the triplets' father.

Because he was holding back just as she was. For self-preservation.

Stop thinking, she ordered herself as she got into her car and turned on the radio, switching the station until she found a catchy song she couldn't resist singing along to. A love song that ended up reminding her of the hot guy taking a shower right now. Grr, why did everything always come back to Reed Barelli?

"So how's married life?" Norah's mother, Arlena, asked as she set a slice of apple pie in front of Reed at the counter of the Pie Diner.

"Things are working out great," Reed said quite honestly.

"It's nice having someone to come home to, isn't it?" Cheyenne said, sidling up with a coffeepot in each hand. She refilled two tables behind them, then poured Reed a fresh cup.

"You two," Shelby chided. "Leave the poor detective alone. We all know theirs isn't a real marriage."

Reed stiffened, glancing at Shelby. Norah's sister was sharp and cautious, a successful business owner, and had held her own against one of the wealthiest and most powerful businessmen in Wedlock Creek, Liam Mercer, whom she'd eventually married. He felt like Shelby was trying to tell him something. Or trying to get across a message. But what?

Their marriage *was* real. They might not be loving and cherishing, but they were honoring each other's deepest wishes and needs.

But still, he couldn't shake what she'd said. *Not a real marriage. Not a real marriage. Not a real marriage.*

If their union wasn't real, then why would he feel such responsibility for her children? And he did. He had from day one when he'd woken up with the wedding ring and seen that photo of Norah and her triplets on the day they were born.

"Well, everyone's happy, including my beloved little grandbabies, so that's what matters," Arlena said, taking away Reed's empty plate.

Cheyenne nodded.

Shelby nodded extra sagely.

Arlena returned with the stroller, parking it beside Reed. "Look who's here to take you home," she cooed to the triplets. She frowned, then looked at him. "What do they call you?"

"Call me?" he repeated.

"Call you," Norah's mother repeated. "Da-da? Papa? Reed? Mama's husband?"

He felt his cheeks sting. Had Norah talked to her mom about their conversation? He doubted there'd been time. "They don't talk yet, so, of course, they don't call me anything."

"They'll be taking any day," she said, clearly uninterested in letting this line of questioning go. He should suggest detective work on the side for Arlena Ingalls.

He swallowed and got up from the bar stool, refusing to take the twenty Cheyenne tried to foist back at him. He put the bill under his empty coffee mug and got out of there fast with the giant stroller. Or as fast as anyone could make their way around tables in a diner while pushing a three-seat stroller with a yellow-and-silver polka-dotted baby bag hanging off the handle.

Anyway, what he'd said in regard to "how married life was" was true: things *were* great. He and Norah had to get used to each other—that was all. Yes, he'd made a mistake in not being clear about the father title, but the subject hadn't come up even though it was really the root and heart of staying married in the first place.

What the hell was wrong with him? How could he be so damned dense sometimes?

And what *were* the triplets going to call him?

He didn't like the idea of them calling him Reed.

Humph.

Frowning again, he settled the babies in their car seats, got the stroller in the trunk of his SUV and drove to the ranch, grateful, as always, that he was making this drive, that he was going home to the ranch. The summer sun lit the pastures through the trees and, as expected, the sight of the homestead relaxed Reed in a way nothing could. He remembered running out to the crazy weeping willow, which always looked haunted, with David Dirk when they were nine, David talking about his uncle who'd just won a quarter million dollars in Vegas and "was so lucky" that their lives were changing. He remembered David saying that if only his mother could win that kind of money, they'd have everything and wouldn't need anything else. As if money alone—

Wait a minute. Reed pulled the car over and stared hard at that weeping willow.

Could David have gone to Las Vegas? To try to win a pot of money to make having multiples more palatable? Or just easier? Or maybe he'd gone there to hide out for a few days before the wedding, to think through what he wanted?

He pulled out his phone and called David's bank. In seconds he was switched over to the manager and reintroduced himself as the detective working on the Dirk disappearance. Reed's predecessor had noted that David hadn't taken out a large sum of cash before he'd gone missing. But David had never been a gambler. He wouldn't risk more than five hundred bucks on slots and tables, even for the chance of a big payday. "Can you tell me if David withdrew around five hundred dollars the week of the tenth?"

"He withdrew two hundred and fifty dollars on the eleventh. Then another hundred on the twelfth."

Well, hardly enough cash for even a cheap flight, a cheap motel and quarters for a few slot machines. But he might have had cash socked away, too.

It was just a hunch. But Reed would bet his ranch that David Dirk was in Vegas, sitting at a slot machine and freaking out about what he was doing—and had done.

Before Norah even got out of her car, she could hear the loud, piercing wails from inside Sara Dirk's house. Screeching babies.

Norah rang the bell and it was a good minute before Sara opened the door, a screaming baby against her chest and frazzled stress etched on her tired face. Behind Sara, Norah could see the other twin crying in the baby swing.

"I thought you could use some easy meals to heat up," Norah said, holding up the bag of pies. "I brought you every kind of pot pie we make at the Pie Diner."

Sara looked on the verge of tears. "That's really nice of you," she managed to say before the baby in her arms let out an ear-splitting wail.

"Could you use a break?" Norah asked, reaching out her arms.

"Oh God, yes," Sara said, handing over the baby girl. "This is Charlotte. And that's Gabrielle," she added, rushing over to the crying one in the swing. She scooped her out and rocked her, and the baby quieted.

Norah held Charlotte against her chest, rubbing the baby's back and murmuring to her.

"A few minutes' reprieve," Sara said. "They like the change, but then they'll start up again."

"Is your husband at work?" Norah asked, giving Charlotte's back little taps to burp her.

Sara nodded. "He works at the county hospital and starts at 5:00 a.m. But the poor guy was up for a couple hours before then. He's such a great dad. He calls and texts as often as he can to check to see if I'm okay, if they're okay."

Norah smiled. "Support is everything."

Sara nodded. "It really is. David's fiancée said she'd come over this morning to help out. I feel so bad for her. Is there still no word on David?"

"Not that I know of."

The doorbell rang and there was Eden, her blond hair in a ponytail. Norah knew Eden from the Pie Diner, like just about everyone in town, so no introductions were necessary. And since David had done his share of dating among the single women in town, Norah's two weeks as David's girlfriend hardly merited a second thought. There wouldn't be any awkwardness in that department with Eden, thank heavens.

Eden burst into tears. "You know what I think?" she asked, taking Gabrielle from Sara and rocking the baby in her arms while sniffling. "I think David up and left. I think he changed his mind about me and didn't want to break my heart. But—" She let out a wail. "He broke it anyway." She cried, holding the baby close against her, her head gentle against Gabrielle's head.

"That man loves you to death," Sara said. "Everyone knows that."

"Well, he's either dead in a ditch somewhere or he left on his own because he doesn't want to marry me," Eden said, sniffling.

Norah handed her a tissue. It wasn't her place to mention Reed's theory. But maybe she could work in the subject of the chapel to see if Eden brought up whether or not David wanted multiples the way she did.

Before Norah could even think about how to pose a question about marrying at the chapel, Eden's phone rang. Sara took Gabrielle as Eden lunged for her phone in her bag, clearly hoping it was her fiancé.

"It's him!" Eden shrieked. "It's David!"

Norah stared at Eden as she screamed, "Hello, Davy

Doo?" into her phone and then realized she should at least pretend to give the woman some privacy.

Eden was listening, her blue eyes narrowing with every passing second, her expression turning murderous. "*What? I was kidding when I got to your cousin's house today and said I was sure you left on your own because of me! I just said that so everyone would say 'Of course that's not true.' But it is!*" she screamed so loudly that both babies startled and stopped fussing entirely.

Whoa boy. So Reed's theory was right.

"Yes, I hear the twins crying again, David. I'm in the same house with them. It's what babies do!" Silence. Eyes narrowing some more. Death expression. And then she said through gritted teeth, "I don't want just *one* baby. I want triplets! Or even quadruplets! Twins at the least!" More listening. More eyes narrowing. "Well, fine! Then I guess we're through!" She stabbed at the End Call button with her finger, threw the phone in her bag, then stormed out. A second later she was back. "I'm sorry you had to hear that. Apparently I was engaged to a weenie twerp! No offense to your husband or his family, Sara," she added, then stormed out again.

Norah stared at Sara, who looked as amazed as Norah felt.

"Omigod," Sara said. "What was that?"

Norah shifted little Charlotte in her arms. "A little miscommunication in expectations before the wedding."

"A little?" Sara shook her head. "And I don't know if I'd classify that as miscommunication. Eden has been talking about getting married at the chapel and having triplets from the first family dinner she was invited to.

David knew what she wanted. He probably didn't think too much about it until his cousin had twins—colicky twins—and he realized what he'd be in for. David has witnessed some whopper arguments between me and my husband. He probably just ran scared with the wedding coming so close."

"Well, I'm glad he's okay—that he wasn't hurt or anything like that," Norah said, realizing something had changed. She gasped—Charlotte had fallen asleep in her arms. She glanced at Sara, who was beaming. Sara pointed to the nursery and Norah tiptoed into the room and laid the baby in her crib. The little creature didn't even stir.

"I owe you," Sara said. "Thank you!"

They glanced at Gabrielle, who was rubbing her eyes and yawning. Easily transferred to the vibrating swing, she, too, was asleep a few seconds later.

"I get to have coffee!" Sara said. "Thank you so much for staying to help."

"Anytime," Norah said. "See you at the next class. Oh, and if your husband hears from David, will you let Reed know?"

"Will do," Sara said.

As Norah headed home, eager to see her own baby multiples, she wondered if she was the one with the problem. She'd picked three men who didn't want to be fathers. She'd dated David, albeit for two weeks. Then her babies' father. Now Reed.

She was chewing that over when she opened the front door to find Reed sitting in the family room with all three babies in their swings, cooing and batting at their little mobiles. He was reading them a story from a brightly colored book with a giraffe on the cover.

Not a father, huh? Sure. The man was father material whether he liked it or not. Knew it or not.

"Have I got news for you," she said and then told him the whole story about Eden and the phone call from David.

Reed shook his head. "At least he's not dead—yet, anyway. Once Eden gets her hands on him…"

"I didn't get the sense he told her where he was or when or if he was coming home."

"I'm ninety-nine percent sure I know where he is— Las Vegas. But it's a big place, and since he's not using his credit cards, he could be at any super-cheap hole-in-the-wall motel. Though now that he's let the cat out of the bag that he's alive and well and afraid of triplets, he might start using his cards and check in somewhere cushy while he lets Eden digest the news."

Not a minute later a call came in from the station. An officer reporting that David Dirk had finally used his MasterCard to check into the fancy Concordia Hotel on the Strip.

"I have to say, Detective. You're good."

"Does that mean you're coming to Vegas with me?" he asked.

Chapter Eleven

Just like that, Norah found herself on a plane to Las Vegas, a city she'd never been to, with Reed beside her, studying the floor plans of the Concordia Hotel and the streets of Vegas on his iPad.

As she stared out at the clouds below, she knew the answer she should have given was "No. Of course not. I'm not going." But what had come out of her mouth, with barely any hesitation was "Yes." This trip wasn't a honeymoon. Or a vacation. But it wasn't strictly business, either. Or Wedlock Creek police business. David Dirk had every right to disappear; once Reed knew for sure that the man had willingly left town, the case had been closed. But Reed wanted to find David and talk to him old friend to old friend. Bring him home. And Norah wanted some time away from real life with her…husband.

Why, she wasn't quite sure. What would be different in a new environment? They were the same people with the same gulf between them.

Still, the trip was a chance. To experience Reed off duty, away from home, where neither of them had any of their usual responsibilities. To see who they were together in a completely different environment. Maybe there would be nothing between them and Norah could just start to accept that their relationship was exactly what she'd agreed to. A platonic marriage slash business partnership for mutual benefit.

The only problem with that was the fact that just sitting this close to Reed, their sides practically touching, she'd never been so aware of a man and her physical attraction to him in her entire life.

"Of course, I booked us separate rooms," Reed said, turning to glance at her. "Right across the hall from each other."

Too bad the Concordia wasn't completely booked except for one small room with a king-size bed, she thought, mesmerized by the dark hair on his forearms and how the sunlight glinted on his gold wedding band, the one that symbolized their union.

Before she knew it, the plane had landed and they were checking in at the front desk, then being shown to their rooms. Reed had 401. Norah was in 402.

"Meet you in the hallway in twenty minutes?" he asked. "I don't have much of a plan to find David other than to sit in the lobby for a while to see if he passes through. We might get lucky. I tried calling David's friend Kyle Kirby, the one who seemed to be withholding, but he didn't answer his phone or my knock at his door. We're gonna have to do this the boring way."

"It's my chance to see you doing surveillance work," she said. "Not boring at all. See you in twenty," she added and hurried inside her room with her weekend bag.

The room was a bit fancier than she'd expected. King-size bed, wall of windows and a fuzzy white robe hanging on the bathroom door. She called her mom to check on the triplets, who were fine and having their snack, then she freshened up and changed into a casual skirt, silky tank top and strappy sandals.

Twenty minutes later, when she went into the hallway, Reed was standing there and she caught his gaze moving up and down the length of her. He liked strappy, clearly. Good.

He was amazingly handsome, as always. He wore dark pants and a dark buttoned shirt, no tie. He looked like a detective.

They sat in the well-appointed lobby for forty minutes, pretending to be poring over maps of the Strip and brochures and dinner menus. No sign of David. Many people came through the lobby, all shapes and sizes and nationalities. Norah noticed a coffee bar across the lobby and had a hankering for an iced mocha. She definitely needed caffeine.

"Want something?" she asked Reed, who was glancing over the lobby, his gaze shooting to the chrome revolving doors every time they spun.

"Iced coffee, cream and sugar. And thanks."

"Coming right up," she said and sauntered off, wondering if he took his eyes off his surveillance to watch her walk away. She turned back to actually check and almost gasped. He *was* watching her. But then he darted his eyes back to the revolving door. Busted!

This meant that no matter what he had to say about ignoring their attraction to each other, he ignored it only when he had to. There was hope to change things between her and the detective. And she was going for it. What happened in Vegas didn't have to stay in Vegas all the time, right?

Her mood uplifted with her secret plan, Norah stood behind a group of women who had very high-maintenance drink orders—double no whip this and no moo that—and studied the board to see if she wanted to try something besides her usual iced mocha when someone said, "Norah?"

She whirled around.

And almost gasped again.

David Dirk himself was staring at her, his mouth agape. "Holy crap, it *is* you," he said, walking over to her. Tall and lanky with light brown hair and round, black glasses, he held an iced coffee in one hand and a small white plate with a crumb cake in the other. "I never took you for a Vegas type."

What did *that* mean? That she couldn't let loose and have fun? Let down the ole hair and have a cocktail or three? Throw away a couple hundred bucks? Okay, maybe fifty at most.

I'm actually here with the detective who's been searching for you for days, she wanted to say. But who knew what David's frame of mind was? He might bolt.

"I'm here with my husband," she said, holding up her left hand and giving it a little wave. She turned and looked toward where Reed was sitting, staring at him hard for a second until she caught his attention. When he looked up and clearly saw David, his eyes practically bugged out of his head.

She turned back to David, who was staring at her ring.

"Oh, wow, congrats!" David said, a genuine smile on his face. "I didn't know you got married. Good for you. And good for your triplets." He bit his lip, looked at the ring again and then promptly burst into tears. He put the drink and the crumb cake down on the counter beside them and slashed each hand under his eyes. "I'm supposed to be getting married tomorrow night. At the chapel," he added, looking stricken.

He sniffled and Norah reached into her bag for her little packet of tissues. He took the whole packet and noisily blew his nose.

"But…?" she prompted, despite knowing exactly what the *but* was.

Tears slipped down his cheeks. Had he always been such a crier? They'd gone to two movies during the two weeks they'd dated, action flicks with very little pathos, so she hadn't had a chance to see him show much emotion.

"I…" He dabbed at his eyes with a wadded-up tissue.

"Whoa, David? David Dirk?" Reed asked with great feigned surprise as he walked up to them.

David stared at Reed, clearly trying to place him. His mouth dropped open, then curved into a grin. "No way. No flipping way! Reed Barelli? Who I last saw when I was thirteen?"

"It's me, man," Reed said, extending his hand.

Instead of taking his hand, David pulled Reed into a hug and sobbed. "You're probably wondering how my

life is after all these years. I'll tell you. It sucks. I've ruined everything. Destroyed the best thing that ever happened to me." He pulled a few tissues from the packet
and dabbed at his eyes again.

"Why don't we go get a beer?" Reed said, his arm
slung around David's shoulders. "We'll catch up." He
turned to Norah. "You'll be all right on your own for a
couple of hours, honey?"

Honey. It was for show, but it warmed her heart none-
theless.

"Sure," she said. "I'll hit the shops. Maybe get a
massage."

"Wait," David said. "*You two* are married? How'd
you even meet?" he asked, looking from Reed to Norah.

"Long story," Reed said. "I'll tell you all about it
over a cold one. And you can fill me in on what's going
on with you."

David nodded, his shoulders slumped. "I let the best
thing that ever happened to me get away."

"There's always a second chance if you don't screw
it up," Reed said as they headed toward the bar.

Here's hoping so, Norah thought. *For everyone.*

The waiter placed two craft beers and a plate of nachos with the works on the square table in front of Reed
and David. David took a chug of his beer, then said,
"Okay, you first. How'd you meet Norah?"

He told David the entire story. The truth and nothing but the truth. He and Norah had talked about being
generally tight-lipped about their story of origin, but
he had a feeling David could use the information and
apply it to himself.

Now it was David's eyes that were bugging out of his head.

"Oh man," David said, chugging more beer. "So you'll get it. You got married at the chapel. And now you're the father of triplets."

There was that word again. *Father.*

"What I can't believe is that you actually proposed *staying* married," David said. "The woman handed you annulment papers, man! You were home free."

"I couldn't just walk away from Norah and the babies. How could I?" He knew he didn't need to add, "You of all people should know that." He was sure David had heard it loud and clear. And from his old friend's expression, Reed was certain.

"I don't want to walk away from Eden," David said. "I love her. I know I screwed up by running away. But I had to think. I had to get my head on straight. Spending time with my cousin and those screaming colicky twins of his made me realize I'm not ready for that. I don't want that."

"You don't want *what*, exactly?" Reed asked. "A colicky baby? Twins? Or kids at all?"

David pulled a nacho onto his plate but just stared at it. "I don't know."

How could such a smart guy know so little? "Why not just tell Eden the truth?"

David frowned. "I did when I called her yesterday. She was so angry at me she hung up." Tears glistened in the guy's eyes and he ate the loaded nacho chip in one gulp.

"I think you should call Eden. FaceTime her, actually. And tell her exactly how you feel. Which sounds to me like you love her very much and want to marry her, but you're not ready for children and certainly not ready for multiples."

"That's it, exactly. I want kids someday. Just not now. And not all at once."

"Tell her. You need to have faith in your relationship with her, David. And remember, that showing her you didn't have faith in her, in your relationship, by running, is probably what is stinging her the most."

David seemed to think about that. He nodded, then took a sip of his beer. "So is it as awful as I think?"

Reed took a swig of his beer. "Is what?"

"Living with three screaming babies."

"Actually, I love those little buggers." The minute he said it, he felt his smile fade. He'd do anything for them. Of course he loved them. He had since the day he'd first upsie-downsied Bea on the rickety porch of Norah's old rental house.

"Really?" David asked, eyes wide behind the black-framed glasses.

"Yeah. Huh. I guess being a father can be more instinctive than I thought. There's really nothing to it other than caring and showing up and doing what needs to be done."

David nodded. "Right. I guess I don't want to do any of that—yet."

Reed laughed. "Then you shouldn't. And don't have to. Not everyone is ready for parenthood at the same time." He thought about Norah, who'd had to be ready. And him, too, in a way. But something told Reed he'd been ready for a long time. Waiting to give his heart to little humans in the way his own father hadn't been willing.

So. He *was* their father. Father. Daddy. He laughed, which made David look at him funny.

"Just thinking about something," Reed said.

David got up and polished off his beer, putting a twenty on the table. "I'm gonna go FaceTime Eden. Wish me luck. I'm gonna need it."

"Go get her," Reed said.

But as he sat there, finishing his beer and helping himself to the pretty good nachos, he realized something that twisted his gut.

Maybe he'd been focusing on the father thing as an excuse not to focus on the marriage thing. Maybe it was only *husband* he had the issue with. *Husband* that he didn't want to be.

Deep down he knew it was true. Of course it was true; it was the whole reason he'd proposed what he'd proposed. A sham of a marriage. So he'd get what he really wanted. His ranch. And a chance to still be the father he'd never had. A chance to do right.

But he also knew deep down that it wasn't what Norah wanted. At all. And she was so independent-minded and used to being on her own that he was pretty sure she wouldn't give up her dreams so soon. She'd tell him the plan wasn't working, that she needed more and she'd hold out for a man who could be a father and a husband.

She deserved that.

Reed sat there long after his beer was gone, his appetite for the nachos ruined. What the hell was going to happen to him and Norah?

* * *

If Norah wasn't mistaken, Reed was being…distant.

While Reed had been with David at the bar, she'd gone into the hotel's clothing boutique and bought herself a little black dress she'd have no use for at home. It wasn't cheap and she'd likely wear it every few years, since it was kind of a classic Audrey Hepburn sleeveless with just the right amount of low neckline to make Norah feel a bit more daring than her usual mom-of-three self.

She and Reed had agreed to meet at six thirty for dinner at an Italian restaurant in their hotel that was supposed to have incredible food. But when she came out of her room at six thirty on the nose, all dolled up, including a light dab of perfume in the cleavage, Reed seemed surprised. And kept his eyes on her face. Not even a peek at her in the hotsy-totsy dress.

Instead, he filled her in on what had happened with David, how he'd texted his old buddy an hour ago to ask if he'd spoken to Eden and how things had gone. David hadn't gotten back to him.

Love, marriage, parenthood, life. Why was it so complicated? Why did wanting one thing mean you had to give up another thing? Compromise was everything in life and relationships.

Can I give up wanting what I used to dream about? she asked herself as they walked into Marcello's, so romantic and dimly lit and full of candles and oil paintings of nudes and lovers that Norah figured Reed hadn't known what they were in for. *Can I stay married to a man I'm falling in love with when it's platonic and he wants to keep it that way forever?*

Maybe not forever. Maybe just till the triplets were grown and off starting their lives and he could finally take a breath from the sense of responsibility he felt. Oh, only eighteen years. No biggie.

Face-palm. Could she live this way for eighteen years?

Norah had just noticed a sign on an easel by the long zinc bar that said Closed For Private Event when a woman rushed up to them. The restaurant was closed? Or the bar?

"Oooh," the woman said, ushering them inside the restaurant "You two had better hurry. There's only one table left. Otherwise you'll have to eat standing at the counter along the back."

Huh? She glanced at Reed, who shrugged, and they followed the hostess to a small round table for two. A man and a woman sat a table on a platform in the center of the dining room, a candle between them, wineglasses and a plate of bruschetta.

Hmm, bruschetta, Norah thought. She definitely wanted some of that. "Maybe it's their anniversary," she told Reed. "And they're high rollers or something, so they get a platform."

"You never know in Vegas," he said, his dark eyes flashing in the dimly lit room. He looked so damned hot, this time all in black, again tieless but wearing a jacket and black shoes.

They were seated and Norah couldn't help but notice the fortyish couple at the table beside theirs. The woman sat with her arms crossed over her chest, looking spitting mad. The man was gobbling up Italian bread and slathering it with butter.

"How can you even eat when I'm this upset!" the woman hiss-whispered.

The man didn't quite roll his eyes, but he didn't stop buttering the bread or popping it in his mouth.

"Welcome!" said the woman at the platform table.

Norah turned her attention to her. She and the man beside her stood. They had microphones. Gulp. This was clearly the "special event." Had she and Reed crashed a wedding or something?

Should they get up now and slink out? While all eyes were focused on the couple and it was dead quiet otherwise?

"We'll slip out when she stops talking, when it's less noticeable," Reed whispered.

Norah nodded. *Awk*ward.

"I know it's not easy for you to be here," the woman continued, turning slowly around the room to speak to all tables. "And because you are here, you've taken the first step in your relationship recovery."

Okay, what? Relationship recovery?

Reed raised an eyebrow and looked at Norah; now it was her turn to shrug.

"My name is Allison Lerner," the woman on the platform said. "My husband, Bill, here, and I have been married for thirty-six years. Yes, we got married at eighteen—*badump!* No, seriously, ladies and gents, we have been married for thirty-six years. Some of those years were so bumpy we threatened each other with divorce every other day. Some months were good. Some days were amazing. Do you want to know *why* we didn't divorce despite the arguments, problems, issues, this, that and the other?"

"Yes!" a woman called out.

Allison smiled. "We didn't divorce because—and this is the big secret—we *didn't want* to. Not really. Even when we hated each other. We didn't want to not be married to each other. Not really."

"What the hell kind of special event is this?" Reed whispered. "They're the entertainment?"

"God, I hope not," Norah whispered back.

"All of you taking tonight's Relationship Recovery seminar are here because you don't want to divorce or separate or go your separate ways, either. So enjoy a glass of wine, folks, order your appetizers and entrées, and once the waiters are off in the kitchen, we'll start the hard work of saving our relationships. Because we want to!"

Norah glanced around. The woman with the arms crossed over her chest had tears in her eyes. Her husband was rubbing her arm—half-heartedly, but hey, at least he was doing something. The entire restaurant must be booked for the seminar.

"I sure got this one restaurant choice wrong," Reed said. "Shall we?" he asked, throwing down his napkin.

"Sir, you can do this," Allison Lerner said from behind them as she put a hand on Reed's arm. She and her husband must have been on the lookout for runners. "You deserve this. You both do. Give yourselves—and your marriage," she added, glancing at their wedding rings, "a chance."

"No, I—" Reed started to say.

"Allison is right," Norah said to Reed. "We need to learn how to fight for our marriage instead of against it."

As Reed gaped at her, she realized how true that

was. Reed was fighting against it without even knowing it because he didn't want a real marriage. Norah was fighting against it because she wanted more when she'd agreed to less. Did that even make sense? No wonder she was so confused about her feelings.

"We need to figure out how to make this work, right?" Norah said. "Let's stay."

Reed stared at her, then glanced at Allison's patiently kind face. He sat back down.

"I'm thinking of pasta," Norah said, opening her menu.

He raised his eyebrow at her. Scowled a bit. Then she saw the acquiescence in his eyes and the set of his shoulders. "Okay, okay. I'm in." He opened his menu.

They ordered a delicious-sounding seafood risotto as an appetizer. Norah chose the four-cheese-and-mushroom ravioli for an entrée; Reed went with the stuffed filetto mignon. Norah sure hoped he'd offer her a bite.

"Everyone, take a sip of your beverage—wine, soda, water, what have you," Bill Lerner said from the platform.

Norah and Reed picked up their glasses, clinked and took a sip. The woman next to them frowned. There was no clinking at their table.

"Okay, now put down your drinks," Bill said. "Turn to your partner. Look at your partner and say the first nice thing that comes to you in reference to your partner. Ladies, you begin."

Norah turned to Reed. This was an easy one. "I love how you are with the triplets. I love how you read to them and blow raspberries on Brody's and Bea's arms but not Bella's because you know she doesn't like it. I love that you know which of them likes sweet potatoes and which hates carrots. I feel like I can relax as a parent in my own home...well, *your* home, for the first time since they were born because you're there. Really, really there. It's a good feeling. Better than I even hoped it would be."

Norah felt tears spring to her eyes. She hadn't meant to say all that. But every word was true. Oh hell. That was the entire reason she'd agreed not to rip up the annulment papers—so that exactly what had happened would happen. And she wanted things to change? She wanted more? She was being selfish. Demanding more of Reed than he wanted to give. Putting the triplets' good new fortune in jeopardy. Mommy's love life had to come second. Period.

Reed took her hand and held it. "Thank you. That means a lot to me. Those babies mean a lot to me."

She almost burst into tears but held back the swell of emotion by taking a sip of wine.

"Okay, gentlemen," Allison said from the platform. "Your turn. Say the first true and nice thing you feel about your partner."

Reed took a sip of his wine and then looked at Norah. "I admire you. You've got your act together. You're lovely. You're kind. You're funny. I like seeing you around the house."

Norah laughed. She liked what he'd said. Maybe it wasn't quite as personal as what she'd said, but it came down to him liking her, really liking her, as a person. And liking having her around.

"Okay, gentlemen," Bill said into the mic. "Now look

at your partner and tell her how you felt about what she said."

Reed put down his glass of wine, which from his expression, he clearly wanted to gulp. "Maybe I am the triplets' father, after all."

Norah did feel tears sting her eyes this time and she didn't wipe them away. She was also speechless.

"I realized it before you said what you said. I realized it from talking to David Dirk. I love those babies, Norah. They have my heart. I am their father. If they'll have me."

Norah bit her lip. "They'll have you." *I'll have you.*

"Okay, ladies, now tell your partner how the nice thing he said about you made you feel."

Norah took Reed's hand and squeezed it. "You'll never say anything that I'll treasure more than what you just did. The triplets come first. That's just how it is with me."

He tilted his head as if considering something. But he didn't say anything. He just nodded.

"Whew!" Allison said from the platform. "That is quite a bit of work we did all before the entrées were served! Feel free to talk about what we just did or change the subject and enjoy dinner. Once you've had a chance to eat, we'll resume with the next exercise. Of course, after dinner, we'll get into the heavy lifting."

"Luckily we've got plans," Reed whispered. "So we'll have to skip the heavy lifting."

Norah smiled. "Oh?"

"There's something I want to show you. Something more fun than heavy lifting."

"I feel like my head was put back on straight," she

said. "So I'd say this Relationship Recovery seminar was a huge success. In just one exercise."

He squeezed her hand but again didn't say anything and cut into his delicious-looking filetto mignon. He cut a bite and instead of lifting the fork to his mouth, reached it out to hers. "Ladies first."

She smiled, feeling her moment-ago resolve to focus on the partnership and not her heart start to waver. How was she supposed to avoid her feelings for Reed Barelli when he was so wonderful?

She took the bite and closed her eyes at how tender and delicious the steak was. "Amazing," she said. "Thank you."

She scooped a ravioli onto his plate. "For you."

And then they ate, drank and didn't talk more about the exercise, which the poor woman at the next table was trying to get her husband to do.

"So you really like my hair this way?" she'd said three times.

The husband shoveled his pasta into his mouth and barely looked up. "Honestly, Kayla, with your hair blonder like that, you look just like you did the day I got the nerve to talk to you after earth science class junior year of high school. Took me a month to get the courage."

The woman gasped and looked like she might faint. Pure joy crossed her face and she reached out her hand and squeezed her husband's. "Oh, Skip."

Sometimes people knew how to say the right things at the right time.

Reed glanced over at the Lerners on the platform. They had their arms linked and were feeding each other fettuccine. Norah's and Reed's plates were practically empty, both of them having just declared they couldn't eat another bite. "I say we slip out now."

Norah smiled. "Let's go."

Reed put a hundred-dollar bill and a fifty on the table, then took her hand and made a point of asking a waiter where the restrooms were, pointing and gesturing for show. They dashed over to the entrance and then quickly ran up the hall. They were free.

"That was unexpected," Norah said on a giggle as they stopped around the corner of the lobby. Her first giggle since her wedding night.

"But worthy," Reed said. "Our marriage feels stronger. We actually did some good work in there."

Norah smiled. "We did. So what did you want to show me?"

"Follow me." He pressed the elevator button. Once they were inside, he pressed the button marked Roof. They rode up forty-two floors and exited into a hallway without any doors except one with a sign that said Roof. Reed pushed open the door and she followed.

It was a roof deck, with couches and chairs and flowers and a bar staffed with a waiter in a tuxedo. Reed took her hand and led her over to the other side of the deck, away from the small groups gathered. She gasped at the view of the Strip, sparkling lights everywhere, all underneath a canopy of stars.

"Something else, huh?" he asked, looking up and then around at the lights.

"Yeah," she said. "Something else. You sure don't see a view like this in Wedlock Creek."

Would she appreciate it even more if Reed were

standing a drop closer? With his arm around her? Or behind her, pressed against her, both of his strong arms wrapped around her? Yes, she would. But hadn't she said she wasn't going to be greedy and selfish? She knew what was important. She had to remember that and not want more.

Reed's phone buzzed in his pocket. He pulled it out and read the screen. "It's David Dirk," he whispered. He turned toward the view. "Hey, David." He listened, then smiled. "Great news. And yes, we'd love to. See you in two hours."

Norah's eyebrows shot up. "We'd love to what?"

"Seems we're invited to be David and Eden's witnesses at their wedding at the Luv U Wedding Chapel."

Norah was surprised. "Wait. Eden flew here? She's giving up the Wedlock Creek chapel and her dream of triplets?"

"I guess she did some soul-searching and decided what she wanted most."

Norah nodded. "That's the key. What you want most. You have to follow that even if it involves some compromise."

And what she wanted most was a good life for her children, the security and safety Reed would provide, the love and kindness, the role model he'd be. She wanted that for her triplets more than she wanted anything. Even if her own heart had to break to get it.

He'd be there, right? Even if he was a million miles away at the same time.

"Wow," Norah said. "She must really love him."

"Well, she's still getting some assurance. Turns out

there's a legend associated with the Luv U Wedding Chapel."

"And what would that be?"

"Eden's parents eloped there the summer after high school, scandalizing both sets of parents. Twenty-five years later the Pearlmans are happy as can be. According to Pearlman family legend, if you marry at the Luv U Wedding Chapel in Las Vegas, you're pretty much guaranteed happily-ever-after."

Norah laughed. "That's a really good legend."

Reed nodded. "This has turned out to be a pretty busy day for us. First a marriage counseling seminar over dinner and now we're witnesses at a legend-inspired wedding that almost didn't happen."

"Like ours," she said. "It's pretty crazy that it happened at all."

He looked into her eyes and squeezed her hand. "I'm glad it did happen, Norah. Our insane wedding changed my life. For the much, much better."

She squeezed his hand back. "Mine, too."

Because I'm in love with my husband. A good thing *and* exactly what wasn't supposed to happen.

I love you, Reed Barelli, she shouted in her head. *I love you!*

She wondered what he was shouting in his head.

Chapter Twelve

"Well, it's not the Wedlock Creek Wedding Chapel," Eden said, reaching for her "something borrowed," her grandmother's seed-pearl necklace. "But if getting married here blessed my parents with twenty-five so-far happy years and four children, I'll take it."

Norah clasped the pretty necklace for Eden and looked at her reflection in the standing mirror in the bridal room of the Luv U Wedding Chapel. The bride looked absolutely lovely in her princess gown with more lace and beading than Norah had ever seen on one dress. "I love it. Your own family legend."

Eden bit her lip and looked at Norah in the mirror. "Do you really believe in the Wedlock Creek legend? I mean, you had triplets without getting married there."

"Well, actually, I did get married there, just after the

fact. So maybe the fates of the universe knew that down the road I'd be getting married at the chapel and so I got my triplets. Just early." She rolled her eyes. "Oh, who the hell knows? I think Reed will tell you the legend is true, though. He got married at the chapel and voilà— father of triplets."

Eden laughed. "Poor guy." Her smile faded as she stared at herself. "Do you think I'm an idiot for forgiving David and marrying him on his terms after what he pulled?"

"I think you know David best and you know what's right and what feels right. No one else can tell you otherwise."

Eden adjusted her long, flowy veil. "I know he loves me. But he did a real bonehead thing just running away. I mean, I *really* thought something happened to him." She frowned. "Maybe he's too immature to get married. I know I'm not about to win Person of the Year or anything, but still."

"Well, he got scared and he didn't know how to deal with it, so he fled. He didn't want to lose you by telling you how he really felt. In the end, though, he did call you and tell you the truth. You two worked it out, because here you are."

Eden's smile lit up her pretty face. "It'll make one hell of a family story, huh? I'll be telling my grandkids about the time Grandpa ran for the hills to avoid having quadruplets."

Norah laughed. "You just might have quadruplets anyway. You never know."

"Mwahaha," Eden said, doing her best evil-laugh impersonation. She turned around to face Norah. "So is this your honeymoon? Is that why you and Reed are here?"

Honeymoons were for real newlyweds. She sighed inwardly. There she went again, wanting more.

Was it wrong to want more when it came to love? If your heart was bursting?

Eden was eyeing her, so she'd better say something reasonable. She had no idea what Reed had told David about the two of them and how they'd ended up married. Probably the truth. She knew Reed Barelli well enough to know that he didn't lie.

"I suppose it's like a mini honeymoon. Reed just started at the police department, so he can't take off any real time." She kind of liked saying that. It was true—in a way. This was like their honeymoon. And since they *were* newlyweds, they should have this time away.

"He must really love you," Eden said, turning back to the mirror to freshen her pink-red lipstick. "He married a single mother of seven-month-old triplets."

Norah felt her heart squeeze. How she wished that were true. Of course, they couldn't go backward and fall in love and then get married. They'd already done the backward thing by getting married first, then actually getting to know each other. She smiled, her heartache easing just a bit. There was hope there, no? If you started out backward, you could only go forward. And forward was love and forever.

Unless your husband was Reed "No Romance" Barelli.

Did a man who didn't believe in romance bring his dry-eyed deal of a wife to see a breathtaking view forty-two flights above the city? Did he do any of the sweet and wonderful things Reed had done? Including offering her the first bite of his incredible filetto mignon?

"He's a great guy," Norah said. He sure was.

Eden smiled and checked that her pearl drop earrings were fastened. "You're so lucky. You have your triplets and your hot new detective husband who's madly in love with you. You have everything."

Oh, if only.

After tearing up a time or two at the wedding and doing her official job as Witness One, Norah watched as David Dirk, looking spiffy in a tuxedo, lifted his bride and carried her out of the Luv U chapel. Reed threw rice and then it was time for the next couple to say their I Do's, so Norah and Reed headed out into the balmy July Las Vegas air.

"Case closed with a happy ending," Reed said. "The best kind of case."

"I think they're going to be just fine," she agreed. "But he'll probably keep doing dumb things."

Reed laughed. "No doubt." He looked over at her. "So should we head back to the hotel? Have a nightcap on the terrace?"

"Sounds good," she said. And too romantic. But there was nothing she'd rather do than continue this night of love and matrimony with her own husband.

They passed a lot of couples holding hands. Brides and grooms with their heads popped out of limo sunroofs, screaming, "I did!" The happy, drunken energy reminded her of her wedding night.

In ten minutes they were back at the Concordia, taking the elevator to the fourth floor. Reed's room was just like hers. The king-size bed in the center of the room had her attention. Suddenly all she could think about was waking up the morning after her wedding, the shock of seeing Fabio-Reed in her bed, half-naked except for the hot, black boxer briefs, the hard planes of his chest and rippling muscles as he shifted an arm, the way his long eyelashes rested on his cheeks.

"Do you think that on our wedding night we…?" She trailed off, staring at the bed.

"We what?"

"Had sex," she said, turning to face him.

He placed his key card on the dresser, took off his jacket and folded it over the desk chair, then went over to the minibar. "No. In fact, I'm ninety-nine percent sure."

"How?"

He poured two glasses of wine from the little bottles. "Because if I made love to you, Norah, I never would have forgotten it." He held her gaze and she felt her cheeks burn a bit, the warmth spreading down into her chest, to her stomach, to her toes.

She took the wineglass he held out and took a sip, then moved over to the windows, unable to stand so close to him or to look directly at him without spontaneously combusting. Being in his room, the bed, images of him, the very thought of his gorgeous face and incredibly hot body… She wanted him with a fierceness she couldn't remember ever experiencing. She wanted to feel his hands and mouth all over her. She wanted him to be her husband—for real.

Maybe she could show him how it could be, how good it could be between them. That if she of all people could let go of mistrust and walls and actually let herself risk feeling something, then he could, too, dammit. There was no way she could be married to this man, share a home and life with him, and not have him in every sense of the word. And the fact that he was clearly attracted to her gave her the cojones to take a long sip of her wine, put down the glass and sit on the edge of the bed.

He was watching her, but he stayed where he was. On the other side of the bed, practically leaning against the wall.

So now what? Should she throw herself at him? No way was she doing that.

Ugh, this was stupid. Forget it. She wasn't going to beg this man—any man—to want her; all of her, heart, mind, soul, body. Hadn't her smart sister told her to let what would happen just happen? She shouldn't be forcing it.

She sighed a wistful sigh and stood. "Well, I guess I'll head to my room, maybe watch a movie. Something funny." She needed funny. A good laugh.

"Sounds good," he said. "I could go for funny." He grabbed the remote control off the desk and suddenly the guide was on the screen. "Hmm, *Police Academy 3*, *Out of Africa*, *Jerry Maguire* or *Full Metal Jacket*?"

Uh-oh. She hadn't meant they watch together. They

were going to lie down on the bed, inches apart, and watch a movie? Really?

"Unless you were hinting that you're sick of me and don't want company," he said with a smile. "I could never get tired of you, so I forget not everyone is dazzled by me 24/7."

She burst out laughing. Hot *and* funny. Who needed the movie? She'd just take him.

"I've seen *Jerry Maguire* at least five times, but you really can't see that enough," she said.

"Really? I've never seen it."

You. Complete. Me, she wanted to scream at him and then grab him down onto the bed and kiss him everywhere on his amazing body.

"Wait, we can't watch a movie without popcorn," he said, picking up the phone. Was the man really ordering from room service? Yes, he was. He asked for a big bowl of popcorn, freshly popped, two sodas, a bottle of a good white wine and two slices of anything chocolate.

Amazing. "You really know how to watch a movie," she said.

He grinned. "The way I see it, you might as well do everything right."

Yup. That was why he hadn't rushed the annulment papers to the county clerk's too-efficient replacement. Because he did things right. Like stay married to a mother of teething seven-month-old triplets who'd lived in a falling-down dump and made her living by the pot pie.

Twenty minutes later, their little movie feast delivered, they settled on the bed, on top of the blanket, the big bowl of popcorn between them, to watch *Jerry Maguire*.

"Oh, it's the *Mission Impossible* dude," he said, throwing some popcorn into his mouth. They were both barefoot and Norah couldn't stop looking at Reed's sexy feet.

"Don't see many movies, huh?" she asked.

"Never really had much time. Hopefully now in Wedlock Creek, I will. Slower pace of life and all that."

She nodded and they settled down to watch. Reed laughed a lot, particularly at the scenes with Cuba Gooding Jr. By the time Renée Zellweger said Tom Cruise had her at hello, Norah was mush and teary-eyed.

"Softy," Reed said, slinging his arm over so that she could prop up against him. She did.

Great. Now they were cuddling. Sort of. His full attention was on the movie. Norah found it pretty difficult to keep her mind on the TV with her head against Reed's shoulder and him stretched out so close beside her. She ate popcorn and dug into the chocolate cake to take her mind off Reed and sex.

But as the credits rolled, Reed turned onto his side to face her. "Do you believe in that 'you complete me' stuff?"

She turned onto her side, too. "Believe in it? Of course I do."

"So someone else can complete you?" he asked. "You're not finished without a romantic partner?"

"What it *means* is that your romantic partner brings out the best in you, makes you realize and understand the depth of your feelings, makes you feel whole in a way you never did before, that suddenly nothing is missing from your life."

He smiled. "I don't know, Norah. I think it was just a good line."

She shook her head. "Nope. She completes him and he knows it."

He reached out to move a strand of hair that had fallen across her face, but instead of pulling his hand back, he caressed her cheek. "You're a true romantic."

"You are, too. You just don't know it," she said. It was so true. Everything he did was the mark of a romantic. His chivalry. His code of honor. His willingness to watch *Jerry Maguire*. The man had ordered popcorn and chocolate cake from room service, for God's sake. He was a romantic.

The thought made her smile. But now he was staring at her mouth.

His finger touched her lip. "Popcorn crumb," he said.

"Does popcorn have crumbs?"

"Yes," he whispered, his face just inches away. He propped up on his elbow and moved another strand of hair away from her face. There was a combination of tenderness and desire in his eyes, in his expression.

He was *thinking*, she realized, fighting the urge to move his head down and kiss her. *Win out, urge*, she telepathically sent to his brain. *Do it. Kiss her. Kiss. Her.*

And then he did. Softly at first. Passionately a second later.

He moved on top of her, his hands in her hair, his mouth moving from her lips to her neck. She sucked in a breath, her hands roaming his back, his neck, his hair. Thick, silky hair. "Tell me to stop, Norah. This is nuts."

"I don't want you to stop. I want you to make love to me."

He groaned and tore off his shirt, then unzipped her dress. She sat up and flung the dress off before he could change his mind. His eyes were on her lacy bra. Her one sexy, black undergarment with panties to match, chosen for this possibility.

And it was happening. Mmm. Yes, it was happening! She lay back, his eyes still on her cleavage. That was good. He was not thinking. He was only feeling. And the moment her hands touched the bare skin of his chest, he was hers. He groaned again and his mouth was on hers, one hand undoing his pants and shrugging out of them while the other unsnapped her bra like a pro.

Suddenly they were both naked. He lay on top of her and propped up on his forearms. "I can't resist you, Norah. I don't have *that* much self-control."

She smiled. "Good."

By the time he reached for the foil-wrapped little packet in his wallet, she was barely able to think for the sensations rocketing every inch, every cell, of her body. But she was vaguely aware that he'd brought a condom. Probably a whole box. Which meant he'd anticipated that something could happen between them.

Her husband *wasn't* lost to her behind that brick wall he'd erected between him and love, him and *feeling*. There was hope for them. That was all she needed to know. In that moment her heart cracked wide-open and let him in fully, risks be damned.

And then he lay on top of her and suddenly they were one, all thought poofing from her head.

Reed's phone was on silent-vibrate, but as a cop he'd long trained himself to catch its hum. He must have drifted off to sleep after two rounds of amazing sex with Norah. His wife. Sex that they weren't supposed to have. Not part of the deal.

He glanced over at her. She lay next to him, turned away on her side, asleep, he figured from her breathing. Her long reddish-brown hair flowed down her sexy bare shoulders. Just looking at her had him stirring once more, wanting her like crazy, but then his phone vibrated again on the bedside table. Then again. And again. What the hell could this be at almost one thirty in the morning?

David Dirk was what it was. A series of texts.

I owe u, man. Good talk we had earlier.

I'm lying here next to my gorgeous wife, feeling so lucky.

I might as well have won a mil downstairs, bruh.

I'm realizing the depth of my love for this woman means she comes 1st.

The selfish crap is stopping. I love Eden 2 death and I'm putting her needs above my own.

Double-date back in the Creek, dude?

Well, good for David Dirk. And Eden. The guy had flipped out, fled town in a spectacularly immature fashion, but had worked it out with himself and laid his heart bare to the woman he loved. And they'd both ended up getting what they'd wanted: each other—still with a hearty dose of legend on their side.

So why was Reed feeling so…unsettled? He put the phone back on the table and lay very still, staring up at the ceiling.

Because he wasn't putting Norah's needs above his own? She wanted the whole shebang—love, romance, snuggles while watching *Jerry Maguire*, a shared, true partnership. And what was he giving her? Just the partnership. Fine, he threw in some snuggles while watching the biggest date-night movie of all time.

And then made mad, passionate love to his wife of "convenience." His life-plan partner.

He shook his head at himself.

He got to feel like a better man than his father was when he was too much of a coward to marry and plan a family of his own. He got to have his ranch when his grandmother would be sorely disappointed at the "marriage" he'd engineered to have the Barelli homestead.

Meanwhile he was keeping Norah from finding what she really wanted. She'd agreed to the marriage deal; she herself had said she wanted nothing to do with love or romance or men. But something had changed for her. Because her heart had opened up. Somehow. Married to a brick wall like him.

Whereas he was still unbreakable and unblastable.

He turned his head and looked at Norah, reaching for a silky strand of her hair. Sex with her was everything he'd thought it would be; they fit perfectly together, they were in rhythm. But afterward, part of him had wanted to hit the streets and just breathe it out. He'd stayed put for her, like he was doing her some kind of big favor. Which had made him feel worse about what he could and couldn't give her.

There was only one thing to do, he realized as he lay there staring back up at the ceiling.

One way out of the mess he'd created by thinking this kind of marriage could work, could be a thing.

Yes. The more he thought about what he needed to do, the more he knew it was the right thing. He'd have to take an hour off work in the morning, but he'd make up the time and then some.

Decision made, he turned over and faced the beige-and-white-striped wallpaper until he realized Norah was a much better sight to fall asleep to. He wanted to reach out and touch her, to wrap his arms around her and tell her how much he cared about her, for her, but he couldn't.

Nothing about Reed Barelli escaped Norah's notice. So she'd caught on to his distance immediately. It had started in the hotel room when she'd woken up five minutes ago. All the warmth from the night before was gone, replaced by this…slight chill. He was polite. Respectful. Offering to run out for bagels or to call room service.

She sat up in bed, pulling the top sheet and blankets up to her chest. *Keep it light, Norah*, she warned herself. "All that hot sex does have me starving," she said with a smile, hoping to crack him.

Instead of sliding back into bed for another round, he practically raced to the phone. "I'll call room service. Omelet? Side of hash browns?"

Deep endless sigh. If she couldn't have him, she may as well eat. She hadn't been kidding. She *was* starving. "Western omelet. And yes to hash browns. And a vat of coffee."

He ordered two of that.

She could still feel the imprint of his lips on hers, all over her, actually. The scent of him was on her. He was all over her, inside her, with her. She felt like Cathy in *Wuthering Heights*—*"I am Heathcliff!"*

Maybe not the most hopeful reference for the Barellis of Wedlock Creek.

"Here you go," he said, handing her the fluffy terry robe, compliments of the Concordia. "Use mine."

Either he didn't want to see her naked anymore or he was just being kind and polite and respectful. She knew it was all the latter. Last night, everything he did had shown how much he'd wanted to see her naked, how much he'd wanted *her*. And now it was all over. Light of day and all that other back-to-Cinderella, back-to-a-pumpkin reality.

They ate on the terrace, making small talk. He asked

how the triplets were, since of course she'd already called to check in on them. They were all fine. The Pie Diner was fine. The police station was fine. Eden and David were fine. Everything was fine but them. What had changed so drastically overnight?

He pushed his hash browns around on his plate. "Norah, we need to talk. Really talk."

Oh hell. She put down her coffee mug. "Okay."

He cleared his throat, then took a long sip of his coffee. Then looked out at the view. Then, finally, he looked at her. "I will stand by you, beside you, and be a father to Bella, Bea and Brody. I want to be their father."

"But…?" she prompted, every nerve ending on red alert.

"But I sense—no, I *know*—that you want more. You want a real marriage. And I'm holding you back from that. If you want to find a man who will be both husband and father, I don't want to hold you back, Norah. You deserve everything."

"I deserve everything, but you won't give me everything," she said, pushing at her hash browns. Anything to avoid directly looking into his eyes.

"I wish I could, Norah. I don't have it in me. I guess it's been too long, too many years of shutting down and out. My job made it easy. I swore off all that stuff, said 'no more,' and I guess I really meant it."

Crud. She wished there was something lying around on the floor of the terrace that she could kick. A soda can. Anything. "So I'm supposed to decide whether I want half a marriage or to let you go so I can find everything in one man."

He glanced out toward the Strip, at the overcast sky. "Yes."

Half of him or the possibility of everything with another? She'd take a quarter of Reed Barelli.

Oh, really, Norah? That's all you deserve? A man who can't or won't give more of himself?

He wanted to serve and protect the community and his family. Same thing to him. She shook her head, trying to make sense of this, trying to make it work for her somehow. But she wasn't a town. She wasn't a bunch of houses or people. She was his *wife*.

"And if I hand you the annulment papers to sign, you're prepared to give up the Barelli ranch? Your heart and soul?"

His expression changed then, but she couldn't quite read it. There was pain, she was pretty sure.

"Yes, I'm fully prepared to give it up."

God. She sucked in a breath and turned away, trying to keep control of herself. "Well, then. If you're willing to give up the ranch that means so much to you, I think we both know we need to get those annulment papers over to the courthouse."

She slid off her wedding ring, her heart tearing in two. "Here," she managed to croak out, handing it to him. "I don't want it."

He bit his lip but pocketed it. Then she pushed out of her chair, ran back into the room, grabbed her clothes off the floor and rushed across the hall into her room.

She sat on the edge of her bed and sobbed.

Chapter Thirteen

"What? You're just gonna let him go?" Aunt Cheyenne said with a frown.

Norah stirred the big pot of potatoes on the stove in the kitchen of the Pie Diner. She'd asked herself that very question on the flight back home and all night in her bedroom at the ranch. Reed had packed a bag and had gone to the one hotel in town to give her "some privacy with your thoughts."

She'd wanted to throw something at him then. But she'd been too upset. When the door had closed behind him, she was just grateful the triplets were with her mother so that she could give in to her tears and take the night to get it out of her system. Come morning, she'd known she'd have to turn into a pot pie baker and a mother and she wouldn't have the time or the luxury of a broken heart.

"Not like I have much choice," she said.

"Uh, Norah, a little more gently with that spoon," her mother said from her station across the kitchen. "The potatoes aren't Reed."

Norah took a deep breath and let up on the stirring. She offered her mom a commiserating smile. "I'll be okay. The potatoes will be okay. The only one who won't be okay is that stubborn brick wall I married by accident."

"Fight for him!" Cheyenne said. "The man is so used to being a lone wolf that he doesn't feel comfortable having a real-life partner. He's just not used to it. But he likes being married or he wouldn't have suggested staying married—no matter what."

Norah had thought of that. Her mind had latched on to so many hopeful possibilities last night. But then she'd come back to all he'd said on the terrace in Las Vegas. "He's giving up the ranch to undo it," Norah reminded her aunt.

"Because he thinks you're losing out," her mother said, filling six pie crusts with the fragrant beef stew she and Cheyenne had been working on this morning. "He wants you to have everything you deserve. The man loves you, Norah."

She shook her head. "If he loved me, he'd love me. And we wouldn't have had that conversation in Vegas." Tears poked her eyes and she blinked them back. The triplets were in the office slash nursery having their nap and she needed to think about them. In Reed, they'd have a loving father but would grow up with a warped view of love and marriage because their parents' lack of love—kisses, romance, the way a committed couple acted—would be absent. They would be roommates, and her children would grow up thinking that was how married people behaved. No sirree.

The super annoying part? She couldn't even go back to the old Norah's ways of having given up on love and romance. Because she'd fallen hard for Reed and she knew she was capable of that much feeling. She did want it. She wanted love. She wanted a father for her babies. She wanted that man to be the same.

She wanted that man to be Reed.

He didn't want to be that man. Or couldn't be. Whatever!

Being Fabio was his fantasy, though, she suddenly realized. A man who *did* want to marry. Fabio had suggested it, after all. Fabio had carried her into that chapel.

Could there be hope?

A waitress popped her head into the kitchen "Norah? There's someone here to see you. Henry Peterfell." The young woman filled her tray with her order of three chicken pot pies and one beef and carried it back out.

"Henry Peterfell is here to see me?" She glanced at her mother and aunt. Henry Peterfell was a pricey attorney and very involved in local government. What could he want with Norah?

She wiped her hands on her apron and went through the swinging-out door into the dining room. Fifty-something-year-old Henry, in his tan suit, sat at the counter, a Pie Diner yellow to-go bag in front of him. "Ah, Ms. Ingalls. I stopped in to pick up lunch and re-

alized I had some papers for you to sign in my briefcase, so if you'd like, you can just John Hancock them
here. Or you can make an appointment to come into
the office. Whatever is more convenient."

Panic rushed into her stomach. "Papers? Am I being
sued?"

Oh God. Was Reed divorcing her? Perhaps he figured they couldn't annul the marriage because they'd
made love. *You're the one who gave him back your ring*,
she reminded herself, tears threatening again. *Of course
he's divorcing you.*

"Sued? No, no, nothing like that." He set his leather
briefcase on the counter and pulled out a folder. "There
are three sets. You can sign where you see the neon
arrow. There, there and there," he said, pointing at the
little sticky tabs.

Norah picked up the papers. And almost fell off the
chair.

"This is a deed," she said slowly. "To the Barelli
ranch."

"Yes," the lawyer said. "Everything is in order. Lovely
property."

"Reed turned the ranch over to me? The ranch is
now mine?"

"That's right. It's yours. Once you sign, of course.
There, there and there," he said, gesturing.

Norah stared at the long, legal-size papers, the black
type swimming before her eyes. *What?* Why would
Reed do this?

"Mr. Peterfell, would it be all right if I held on to
these to read first?"

"Absolutely," he said. "Just send them to my office or drop them off at your convenience."

With that, he and his briefcase of unexpected documents were gone.

Reed had deeded the ranch to her. His beloved ranch. The only place that had ever felt like home to him.

Because he didn't feel he deserved it now that they were going to split up? That had to be the reason. He wasn't even keeping it in limbo in case he met someone down the road, though. He was that far gone? That sure he was never going to share his heart with anyone?

A shot of cold swept through her at the thought. How lonely that would be.

She wasn't letting him get away that easily. Her aunt and mother were right. She was going to fight for him. She was going to fight for Fabio. Because there was a chance that Reed did love her but couldn't allow himself to. And if the feeling was there, she was going to pull it out of him till he was so happy he made people sick.

The thought actually made her smile.

Reed stood in the living room of his awkward rental house—the same old one, which of course was still available because it was so blah—trying to figure out why the arrangement of furniture looked so wrong. Maybe if he put the couch in front of the windows instead of against the wall?

This place would never look right. Or feel right. Or be home.

But giving Norah the ranch had been the right thing to do. Now she'd have a safe place to raise the triplets with enough room for all of them, fields to roam in, and she'd own it free and clear. She'd never have to worry about paying rent again, let alone a mortgage or property taxes—he'd taken care of that in perpetuity.

And he had a feeling his grandmother was looking down at him, saying, *Well, you tried. Not hard enough, but you tried and in the end you did the right thing. She should have the ranch, you dope.*

He *was* a dope. And Norah should have the ranch.

The doorbell rang. He had a feeling it was Norah, coming to tell him she couldn't possibly accept the ranch. Well, tough, because he'd already deeded it to her and it was hers. He'd even talked over the legalities with his lawyer; he'd married, per his grandmother's will, and the ranch was his fair and square. His to hand over.

He opened the door and it was like a gut punch. Two days ago they'd still had their deal. Two nights ago they'd been naked in bed together. And then yesterday morning, he'd turned back into the Reed he needed to be to survive this thing called life. Keeping to himself. No emotional entanglements.

And yet his first day in town he'd managed to get married and become a father to three babies. He was really failing at no emotional entanglements.

"I can't accept this, Reed," she said, holding up a legal-size folder.

"You have no choice. It's yours now. The deed is in your name."

She scowled. "It's your home."

"I'd rather you and the triplets have it. My grandmother would rather that, too. I have no doubt."

"So you get married, get your ranch and then give up the ranch, but the wife who's not really your wife gets to *keep* the ranch. That makes no sense."

"Does anything about our brief history, Norah?" An image floated into the back of his mind, Fabio and Angelina hand in hand, him scooping her up and carrying her into the chapel with its legend and sneaky, elderly caretakers slash officiants.

She stared at him hard. "I'll accept the ranch on one condition."

He raised an eyebrow. "And that would be?"

"I need your help for my multiples class. I'd like you to be a guest speaker. Give the dad's perspective."

No, no, no. What could *he* contribute? "I've only been a dad for a little while," he said. "Do I really have anything to truly bring to the class? And now with things so...up in the air between us."

Up in the air is good, she thought. Because it meant things could go her way. Their way. The way of happiness.

"You have so much to contribute," she said. "Honestly, it would be great if you could speak at all the remaining classes," she said. "Lena Higgins—she's the one expecting all boy triplets—told me her husband wasn't sure he felt comfortable at the class last week and might not be joining her for the rest because the class seemed so mom-focused. Poor Lena looked so sad. A male guest speaker will keep some of the more reluctant dads and caregivers comfortable. Especially when it's Reed Barelli, detective."

He didn't quite frown, so that was something. "I don't know, Norah. I—"

"Did you see how scared some of those dads looked?" she asked. "For dads who are shaking over the responsibility awaiting them—you could set their minds at ease. I think all the students will appreciate the male perspective."

Some of the guys in the class, which had included fathers, fathers-to-be and grandfathers, had looked like the ole deer in the headlights. One diaper was tough on some men who thought they were helpless. Two, three, even four diapers at the same time? Helpless men would poof into puddles on the floor. He supposed he could be a big help in the community by showing these guys they weren't helpless, that they had the same instincts—and fears—as the women and moms among them.

Step up, boys, he thought. That would be his mission.

Ha. He was going to tell a bunch of sissies afraid of diaper wipes and onesies and double strollers to step up when he couldn't step up for the woman he'd do anything for?

Anything but love, Reed?

He shook the thought out of his weary brain. His head ran circles around the subject of his feelings for Norah. He just couldn't quite get a handle on them. Because he didn't want to? Or because he really was shut off from all that? Done with love. Long done.

She was tilting her head at him. Waiting for an answer.

"And if I do this, you'll accept the ranch as yours?" he said.

She nodded.

He extended a hand. "Deal."

She shook his hand, the soft feel of it making him want to wrap her in his arms and never let her go.

"We make a lot of deals," she said. "I guess it's our thing."

He smiled. "The last one failed miserably." He failed miserably. Or had Norah just changed the rules on him by wanting more? They'd entered their agreement on a handshake, too. He wasn't really wrong here. He just wasn't…right.

"This one has less riding on it," she said. "You just have to talk about how you bonded with the triplets. How you handle changing time. Feeding time. Bedtime. What's it like to come home from work and have three grumpy, teething little ones to deal with. How you make it work. How it's wonderful, despite everything hard about it. How sometimes it's not even hard."

He nodded and smiled. "I'll be there," he said. He frowned, his mind going to the triplets. "Norah, how are things going to work now? I mean, until you find the right man, I want to be there for you and the babies. I want to be their father."

"Until I find a father who can be that and a real husband?"

"Okay, it's weird, but yes."

She frowned. "So you're going to get all enmeshed in their lives, give a hundred percent to them, and then I meet someone who fits the bill and you'll just back off? Walk away? Bye, triplets?"

Hey, wait a minute.

"Look, Norah, I'm not walking away from anything. I want to be their father. I told you that. But I want you to have what you need, too. If I can't be both and someone else can…"

Someone else. Suddenly the thought of another man touching her, kissing her, doing upsie-downsie with his babies…

His babies. Hell. Maybe he should back off now. Or he'd really be done for. Maybe they both needed a break from each other so they could go back to having what they wanted. Which was all messed up now.

She lifted her chin. "Let's forget this for now. Anytime you want to see Bella, Bea and Brody, you're welcome over. You're welcome at the ranch anytime."

He nodded, unable to speak at the moment.

She peered behind him, looking around the living room. "The couch should go in front of the windows. And that side table would be better on that wall," she said, pointing. "The mirror above the console table is too low. Should be slightly above eye level."

"That should help. Thank you. I can't seem to get this place right."

"I'm not sure I want it to feel right," she said. "Wait, did I say that aloud?" She frowned again. "Everything is all wrong. I don't like that you left your home, Reed. That place is your dream."

"That place is meant for a family. I want you to have it."

She looked at him for a long moment. He could see her shaking her head without moving a muscle. "See you in class."

He watched her walk to her car. The moment she got in, he felt her absence and the weight of one hell of a heavy heart.

Chapter Fourteen

Word had spread that Detective Reed Barelli, who'd become de facto father to the Ingalls triplets by virtue of marrying their mother at the Wedlock Creek chapel with its Legend of the Multiples, would be a guest speaker at tonight's zero-to-six-month multiples class. There were more men than women this time, several first-timers to the class who practically threw checks at Norah. At this rate, she'd be raking it in as a teacher.

She hadn't even meant to invite him to speak—especially not as a condition of her keeping the ranch. The sole condition, no less. But it had been the best she could come up with, just standing there, not knowing what to say, how to keep him, how to get him to open up the way she had and accept the beautiful thing he was being offered: love. She did want him to be a speaker in her class, and it would get them working together, so that was good. She couldn't try to get through to him if they were constantly apart now that he'd moved out.

They hadn't spent much time together in three days.

He'd come to the ranch to see the triplets every day since their return from Las Vegas. He'd help feed them, then read to them, play with them. Blow raspberries and do upsie-downsies. And then he'd leave, taking Norah's heart with him.

Now here he was, sitting in the chair beside her desk with his stack of handouts, looking so good she could scream.

"Welcome, everyone! As you may have heard through the grapevine, tonight we have a guest speaker. Detective Reed Barelli. When Reed and I got married, he became the instant father of three seven-month-old teething babies. Was he scared of them? Nope. Did he actually want to help take care of them? Yes. Reed had never spent much time around babies and yet he was a natural with my triplets. Why?"

She looked at Reed and almost didn't want to say why. Because it proved he could pick and choose. The triplets. But not her.

She bit back the strangled sob that rose up from deep within and lifted her chin. She turned back toward the class. "Because he wanted to be. That is the key. He *wanted* to be there for them. And so he was. And dads, caregivers, dads-to-be, grandfathers, that's all you have to know. That you want to be there for them. So, without further ado, here is Detective Reed Barelli."

He stood, turned to her and smiled, then addressed

the class. "That was some introduction. Thank you, Norah."

She managed a smile and then sat on the other side of the desk.

"Norah is absolutely right. I did want to be there for the triplets. And so I was. But don't think I had a clue of how to take care of one baby, let alone three. I know how to change a diaper—I think anyone can figure that out. But the basics, including diapers and burping and sleep schedules and naps? All that, you'll learn here. What you won't learn here, or hell, maybe you will because I'm talking about it, is that taking care of babies will tell you who you are. Someone who steps up or someone who sits out. Be the guy who steps up."

A bunch of women stood and applauded, as did a few guys.

"Is it as easy as you make it sound?" Tom McFill asked. "My wife is expecting twins. I've never even held a baby before."

"The first time you do," Reed said, "everything will change. That worry you feel, that maybe you won't know what you're doing? It'll dissipate under the weight of another feeling—a surge of protection so strong that you won't know what hit you. All you'll know is that you're doing what needs to be done, operating by instinct and common sense, Googling what you don't know, asking a grandmother. So it's as hard and as easy as I'm making it sound."

A half hour later Norah took over, giving tutorials on feeding multiples, bathing multiples and how to handle sleep time. Then there was the ole gem: what if both babies, or three or four, all woke up in the middle of the night, crying and wet and hungry. She covered that, watching her students taking copious notes.

Finally the class was over. Everyone crowded around Reed, asking him questions. By the time the last student left and they were packing up to go, it was a half hour past the end of the class.

"You were a big hit," she said. "I knew I called this one right."

"I'm happy to help out. I knew more than I thought on the subject. I'd stayed up late last night doing research, but I didn't need to use a quarter of it."

"You had hands-on training."

"I miss living with them," he said, and she could tell he hadn't meant to say that.

She smiled and let it go. "Most people would think you're crazy."

"I guess I am."

Want more, she shouted telepathically. *Insist on more! You did it with the babies, now do it with me. Hot sex every night, fool!* But of course she couldn't say any of that. "Well, I'd better get over to the diner to pick up the triplets."

"They're open for another half hour, right? I could sure go for some beef pot pie."

She stared at him. Why was he prolonging the two of them being together? Because he wanted to be with her? Because he really did love the triplets and wanted to see them?

Because he missed her the way she missed him?

"I have to warn you," she said as they headed out.

"My family might interrogate you about the state of our marriage. Demand to know when we're patching things up. *If* we will, I should say."

"Well, we can't say what we don't know. That goes for suspects and us."

Humph. All he had to do was say he'd be the one. The father and the husband. It was that easy!

On the way to their cars, she called her mom to let her know she and Reed would be stopping in for beef pot pies so they'd be ready when they arrived. Then she got in her car and Reed got in his. The whole time he trailed her in his SUV to the Pie Diner, she was so aware of him behind her.

The diner was still pretty busy at eight thirty-five. Norah's mom waved them over to the counter.

"Norah, look who's here!"

Norah stared at the man sitting at the counter, a vegetable pot pie and lemonade in front of him. She gasped as recognition hit. "Harrison? Omigod, Harrison Atwood?" He stood and smiled and she threw her arms around him. Her high school sweetheart who'd joined the army and ended up on the east coast and they'd lost contact.

"Harrison is divorced," Norah's mom said. "Turns out his wife didn't want children and he's hoping for a house full. He told me all about it."

Norah turned beet red. "Mom, I'm sure Harrison doesn't want the entire restaurant knowing his business."

Harrison smiled. "I don't mind at all. The more people know I'm in the market for a wife and children, the better. You have to say what you want if you hope to get it, right?"

Norah's mother smiled at Norah and Reed, then looked back at Harrison. "I was just telling Harrison how things didn't work out between the two of you and that you're available again. The two of you could catch up. High school sweethearts always have such memories to talk over."

Can my face get any redder? Norah wondered, shooting daggers at her busybody mother. What was she trying to do?

Get her settled down, that was what. First Reed and now a man she hadn't seen in ten years.

Norah glanced at Reed, who seemed very stiff. He was stealing glances at Harrison every now and then.

Harrison had been a cute seventeen-year-old, tall and gangly, but now he was taller and more muscular, attractive, with sandy-brown hair and blue eyes and a dimple in his left cheek. She'd liked him then, but she'd recognized even then that she hadn't been in love. To the point that she'd kept putting him off about losing their virginity. She'd wanted her first time to be with a man she was madly in love with. Of course, she'd thought she was madly in love with a rodeo champ, but he'd taken her virginity and had not given her anything in return. She'd thought she was done with bull riders and then, wham, she'd fallen for the triplets' father. Maybe she'd never learn.

"Harrison is a chef. He studied in Paris," Aunt Cheyenne said. "He's going to give us a lesson in French cooking. Isn't that wonderful? You two must have so much in common," she added, wagging a finger between Norah and Harrison.

"Well, I'd better get going," Reed said, stepping back. "I have cases to go over. Nice to see you all."

"But, Reed, your pot pie just came out of the oven," Norah's mother said. "I'll just go grab it."

Norah watched him give Harrison the side-eye before he said, "I'll come with you. I want to say goodnight to the triplets."

"They are so beautiful," Harrison said with so much reverence in his voice that Norah couldn't help the little burst of pride in her chest. Harrison sure was being kind.

Reed narrowed his gaze on the man, scowled and disappeared into the kitchen behind her mother.

And then Aunt Cheyenne winked at Norah and smiled. Oh no. Absolutely not. She knew what was going on here. Her mother and aunt realized they had Norah's old boyfriend captive at the counter and had been waiting for Norah and Reed to come in so they could make Reed jealous! Or, at least, that was how it looked.

Sneaky devils.

But they knew Reed wasn't in love with her and didn't want a future with her. So what was the point? Reed would probably push her with Harrison, tell her to see if there was anything to rekindle.

But as cute and nice as Harrison was, he wasn't Reed Barelli. No one else could be.

Every forkful of the pot pie felt as if it weighed ten pounds in his hand. Reed sat on his couch, his lonely dinner tray on the coffee table, a rerun of the baseball game on the TV as a distraction from his thoughts.

Which were centered on where Norah was right now. *Probably on a walking date with Harrison*, he said in his mind in a singsong voice. High school sweethearts would have a lot to catch up on. A lot to say. Memories. Good ones. There were probably a lot of firsts between them.

Reed wanted to throw up. Or punch something.

Just like that, this high school sweetheart, this French chef, would waltz in and take Reed's almost life. His wife, his triplets. His former ranch, which was now Norah's. A woman who wanted love and romance and a father for her babies might be drawn to the known— and the high school sweetheart fit that bill. Plus, they had that cooking thing in common. They might even be at the ranch now, Harrison standing behind Norah at the stove, his arms around her as he showed her how to Frenchify a pot pie. You couldn't and shouldn't! Pot pies were perfect as they were, dammit.

Grr. He took a swig of his soda and clunked it down on the coffee table. What the hell was going on here? He was jealous? Was this what this was?

Yes. He was jealous. He didn't want Norah kissing this guy. Sleeping with this guy. Frenchifying pot pies with this guy.

He flung down his fork and headed out, huffing into his SUV. He drove out to the ranch, just to check. And there was an unfamiliar car! With New York plates!

Hadn't Norah's mother said Harrison had lived on the east coast?

He was losing her right now. And he had let it happen.

This is what you want, dolt. You want her to find everything in one man. A father for her triplets. A husband for herself. Love. Romance. Happiness. Forever. You don't want that. So let her go. Let her have what she always dreamed of.

His heart now weighing a thousand pounds, he turned the SUV around and headed back to his rental house, where nothing awaited him but a cold pot pie and a big, empty bed.

"Upsie-what?" Harrison said, wrinkling his nose in the living room of the Barelli ranch. Correction. The Ingalls ranch. The Norah Ingalls ranch.

Norah frowned. "Upsie-downsie," she repeated. "You lift her up, say 'Upsie' in your best baby-talk voice, then lower her with a 'downsie'!"

They were sitting on the rug, the triplets in their Ex-ersaucers, Bella raising her hands for a round of upsie-downsie. But Harrison just stared at Bella, shot her a fake smile and then turned away. Guess not everyone liked to play upsie-downsie.

Bella's face started to scrunch up. And turn red. Which meant any second she was about to let loose with a wail. "Waaaah!" she cried, lifting her arms up again.

"Now, Bea, be a good girl for Uncle Harrison," he said. "Get it, *Bea* should *be* a good girl. LOL," he added to no one in particular.

First of all, that was Bella. And did he just LOL at his own unfunny "joke"? Norah sighed. No wonder she hadn't fallen in love with Harrison Atwood in high school. Back then, cute had a lot to do with why she'd liked him. But as a grown-up, cute meant absolutely nothing. Even if a man looked like Reed Barelli.

"I'd love to take you out to a French place I know over in Brewer," he said. "It's not exactly Michelin-starred, but come on, in Wyoming, what is? I'm surprised you stuck around this little town. I always thought you'd move to LA, open a restaurant."

"What would give you that idea?" she asked.

"You used to talk a lot about your big dreams. Wanting to open Pie Diners all across the country. You wanted your family to have your own cooking show on the Food Network. Pot pie cookbooks on the *New York Times* bestseller list."

Huh. She'd forgotten all that. She did used to talk about opening Pie Diners across Wyoming, maybe even in bordering states. But life had always been busy enough. And full enough. Especially when she'd gotten pregnant and then when the triplets came.

"Guess your life didn't pan out the way you wanted," Harrison said. "Sorry about that."

Would it be wrong to pick up one of the big foam alphabet blocks and conk him over the head with it?

"My life turned out pretty great," she said. *I might not have the man I love, but I have the whole world in my children, my family, my job and my little town.*

"No need to get defensive," he said. "Jeez."

God, she didn't like this man.

Luckily, just then, Brody let loose with a diaper explosion, and Harrison pinched his nostrils closed. "Oh boy. Something stinks. I guess this is my cue to leave. LOL, right?"

"It was good to see you again, Harrison. Have a great rest of your life."

He frowned and nodded. "Bye." He made the mistake of removing his hand from his nose, got a whiff of the air de Brody and immediately pinched his nostrils closed again.

She couldn't help laughing. "Buh-bye," she said as he got into his car.

She closed the door, her smile fading fast. She had a diaper to change. And a detective to fantasize about.

Chapter Fifteen

Reed kept the door of his office closed the next morning at the police station. He was in no mood for chitchat and Sergeant Howerton always dropped in on his way from the tiny kitchen to talk about his golf game and Officer Debowski always wanted to replay any collars from the day before. Reed didn't want to hear any of it.

He chugged his dark-brew coffee, needing the caffeine boost to help him concentrate on the case he was reading through. A set of burglaries in the condo development. Weird thing was, the thief, or thieves, was taking unusual items besides the usual money, jewelry and small electronics. Blankets and pillows, including throw pillows, had been taken from all the hit-up units.

Instead of making a list of what kind of thief would go for down comforters, he kept seeing Norah and the high school sweetheart with their hands all over each other. Were they in bed right now? He had to keep blinking and squeezing his eyes shut.

He wondered how long the guy had stayed last night. Reed should have made some excuse to barge in and interrupt them a bunch of times. Checking on the boiler or something. Instead, he'd reminded himself that the reason the French chef was there was because of Reed's own stupidity and stubbornness and inability to play well with others. Except babies.

He slammed a palm over his face. Were they having breakfast right now? Was Norah in his button-down shirt and nothing else? Having pancakes on the Barelli family table?

Idiot! he yelled at himself. *This is all your fault.* He'd stepped away. He'd said he couldn't. He'd said he wouldn't. And now he'd lost Norah to the high school sweetheart who wanted a wife and kids. They were probably talking about the glory days right now. And kissing.

Dammit to hell! He got up and paced his office, trying to force his mind off Norah and onto a down-feather-appreciating burglar. A Robin Hood on their hands? Or maybe someone who ran a flea market?

He's going to give us lessons in French cooking, Norah's mother had said. Suddenly, Reed was chopped liver to the Ingalls women, having been replaced by the beef bourguignon pot pie.

So what are you going to do about this? he asked himself. *Just let her go? Let the triplets go? You're their father!*

And he was Norah's husband. Husband, husband,

husband. He tried to make the word have meaning, but the more it echoed in his head, the less meaning it had. Husband meant suffering in his memories. His mother had had two louses and his grandfather had been a real doozy. He thought of his grandmother trying to answer Reed's questions about why she'd chosen such a grouch who didn't like anyone or anything. She'd said that sometimes people changed, but even so, she knew who he was and, despite his ways, he'd seemed to truly love her and that had made her feel special. She'd always said she should have known if you're the only one, the exception, there might be a problem.

So what now? Could he force himself to give this a real try? Romance a woman he had so much feeling for that it shook him to the core? Because he was shaken. That much he knew.

His head spinning, he was grateful when his desk phone rang.

"Detective Barelli speaking."

"Reed! I'm so glad I caught you. It's Annie. Annie Potterowski from the chapel. Oh dear, I'm afraid there's a bit of a kerfuffle concerning your marriage license. Could you come to the chapel at ten? I've already called Norah and she's coming."

"What kind of kerfuffle?" he asked. What could be more of a kerfuffle than their entire wedding?

"I'll explain everything when you get here. 'Bye now," she said and hung up.

If there was one good thing to come from this kerfuffle, it was that he knew Norah would be apart from the high school sweetheart, even for just a little while.

* * *

"Annie, what on earth is going on?" Norah asked the elderly woman as she walked into the chapel, pushing the enormous stroller.

"Look at those li'l dumplings!" Abe said, hurrying over to say hello to the triplets. He made peekaboo faces and Bea started to cry. "Don't like peekaboo, huh?" Abe said. "Okay, then, how about silly faces?" He scrunched up his face and stuck out his tongue, tilting his head to the left. Bea seemed to like that. She stopped crying.

"I'm just waiting for Detective Barelli to arrive," Annie said without looking at Norah.

Uh-oh. What was this about?

"Ah, there he is," Annie said as Reed came down the aisle to the front of the chapel.

Reed crossed his arms over his chest. "About this kerfuffle—"

"Kerfuffle?" Norah said. "Anne used the words *major problem* when she called me."

Annie bit her lip. "Well, it's both really. A whole bunch of nothing, but a lot of something."

Reed raised an eyebrow.

"I'll just say it plain," Abe said, straightening the blue bow-tie that he wore almost every day. "You two aren't married. You spelled your names wrong on the marriage license."

"What?" Norah said, her head spinning.

"The county clerk's temporary replacement checked her first week's work, just in case she made rookie errors, and discovered only one. On your marriage license. She sent back the license to you and Reed and to the chapel, since we officiated the ceremony. You didn't receive your mail yet?"

Had Norah even checked the mail yesterday? Maybe not.

"I was on a case all day yesterday and barely had time to eat," Reed said. "But what's this about spelling our names wrong?"

Anne held up the marriage license. "Norah, you left off the *h*. And, Reed, you spelled your name *R-e-a-d*. I know there are lots of ways to spell your name, but that ain't one of them."

"Well, it's not like you didn't know we were drunk out of our minds, Annie and Abe!" Norah said, wagging a finger at them.

"I didn't think to proofread your names, for heaven's sake!" Annie said, snorting. "Now we're supposed to be proofreaders, too?" she said to Abe. "Each wedding would take hours. I'd have to switch to my reading glasses, and I can never find them and—"

"Annie, what does this mean?" Reed asked. "You said we're not married. Is that true? We're not married because our names were spelled wrong?"

"Your legal names are not on that document or on the official documents at the clerk's office," Abe said.

"So we're not married?" Norah repeated, looking at Reed. "We were never actually married?"

"Well, double accidentally, you were," Annie said. "The spiked punch and the misspelling. You were married until the error was noted by the most efficient county clerk replacement in Brewer's history."

I'm not married. Reed is not my husband.

It's over.

Her stomach hurt. Her heart hurt. Everything hurt.

Reed walked over to Norah and seemed about to say something. But instead he knelt down in front of the stroller. "Hey, little guys. I miss you three."

Brody gave Reed his killer gummy smile, three tiny teeth poking up.

She glanced at his hand. He still wore his wedding ring even though she'd taken hers off. Guess he'd take it off now.

"We'll leave you to talk," Annie said, ushering Abe into the back room.

Norah sat in a pew, a hand on the stroller for support. She wasn't married to Reed. How could she feel so bereft when she never really had a marriage to begin with?

"We can go back to our lives now," she said, her voice catching. She cleared her throat, trying to hide what an emotional mess she was inside. "I'll move out of the ranch. Since we were never legally married, I'm sure that affects possession of the ranch. You can't deed me something you didn't rightfully inherit."

She was babbling, talking so she wouldn't burst into tears.

He stood, giving Bea's hair a caress. "I guess Harrison will be glad to hear the news."

"Harrison?"

"Your high school sweetheart," he said. "The one you spent the night with."

She narrowed her eyes at him. "What makes you think we spent the night together?"

"I drove by the house to see if his car was there."

"Why? Why would you even care? You don't have feelings for me, Reed."

He looked away for a moment, then back at her. "I have a lot of feelings for you."

"Right. You feel responsible for me. You care about me. You're righting wrongs when you're with me."

He shook his head but didn't say anything.

"I should get back to work," she said.

"Me, too," he said.

She sucked in a breath. "I guess when we walk out of here, it's almost like none of it ever happened. We were never really married."

"I felt married," he said. Quite unexpectedly.

"And you clearly didn't like the feeling." She waited a beat, hoping he'd say she was wrong.

She waited another beat. Nothing.

"There's nothing between me and Harrison," she said without really having to. What did it matter to Reed anyway? His urge to drive by the ranch had probably been about him checking up on her, making sure she'd gotten back okay, the detective in him at work. "He did come over for a bit and was so insufferable I couldn't wait for him to leave."

He looked surprised. "But what about all the firsts you two shared?"

"Firsts? I had my first kiss with someone else. I lost my virginity to someone else. I did try sushi for the first time with Harrison. I guess that counts."

"So you two are *not* getting back together," he said, nodding.

"We are definitely not."

"So my position as father of the triplets still stands."

"That's correct," she said even though she wanted to tell him no, it most certainly did not. This was nuts. He was going to be their father in between semi-dates and short-term relationships until the real thing came along for her?

"I'd like to spend some time with them after work, if that's all right," he said. "I have presents for them for their eight-month birthday."

Her heart pinged. "It's sweet that you even know that."

"You only turn eight months once," he said with a weak smile.

And you find a man like Reed Barelli once in a lifetime, she thought. *I had you, then lost you, then didn't ever really have you, and now there's nothing.* Except his need to do right by the triplets, be for them what he'd never had.

"Time to go, kiddos," she said, trying to inject some cheer in her voice. "See you later, then," she said, wondering how she'd handle seeing him under such weird circumstances. Were they friends now?

"I'll get the door," he said, heading up the aisle to open it for her. He couldn't get rid of her fast enough.

Her heart breaking in pieces, she gripped the stroller and headed toward the Pie Diner, knowing she'd never get over Reed Barelli.

"Your grandmother would have loved Norah."

Reed glanced up at the voice. Annie Potterowski was walking up the chapel aisle toward where he sat in a pew in the last row. He'd been sitting there since Norah had left, twenty minutes or so. He'd married her in this place. And been unmarried to her here. He couldn't seem to drag himself out.

"Yeah, I think she would have," Reed said.

Annie sat beside him, tying a knot in the filmy pink scarf around her neck. "Now, Reed, I barely know you. I met you a few times over the years when you came to visit Lydia. So I don't claim to be an expert on you or anything, but anyone who's been around as long as I have and marries people for a living knows a thing or two about the human heart. Do you want to know what I think?"

He did, actually. "Let me have it."

She smiled. "I think you love Norah very much. I think you're madly in love with her. But this and that happened in your life and so you made her that dumb deal about a partnership marriage."

He narrowed his eyes at her. "How'd you know about that?"

"I listen, that's how. I pick up things. So you think you can avoid love and feeling anything because you were dealt a crappy hand? Pshaw," she said, adding a snort for good measure. "We've all had our share of bad experiences."

"Annie, I appreciate—"

"I'm not finished. You don't want to know the up-bringing I had. It would keep you up at night feeling sorry for me. But when Abe Potterowski came calling, I looked into that young man's eyes and heart and soul, and I saw everything I'd missed out on. And so I said yes instead of no when I was scared to death of my feelings for him. And it was the best decision I ever made."

He took Annie's hand in his and gave it a gentle squeeze.

"I was used to shutting people out," she continued. "But you have to know when to say yes, Reed. And your grandmother, God bless her sweet soul, only ever wanted you to say yes to the right woman. Don't let her get away." Annie stood and patted his shoulder. "Your grandmother liked to come in here and do her thinking. She sat in the back row, too, other end, though."

With that, Annie headed down the aisle and disappeared into the back room.

Leaving Reed to do some serious soul-searching.

Chapter Sixteen

"Not married?" Shelby repeated, her face incredulous as she cut up potatoes for the lunch-rush pot pies.

Norah shook her head, recounting what Annie and Abe had said.

"Oh hell," her mother said. "I really thought you two would work it out."

"You pushed Harrison on me last night!" Norah complained even though she knew why.

"Yeah, but I only did that because he was here when you called and said you and Reed were stopping in for pot pies. I wanted Reed to know he had competition for your heart."

"Well, he doesn't. Harrison was awful. He freaked the minute one of the triplets did number two in his presence."

"Norah, you and Reed belong together," Aunt Cheyenne said as she filled six pie tins with beef stew. "We can all see that."

"I thought we did," Norah said, tears threatening her eyes. "But he never wanted a real relationship. He wanted to save me. And he wanted the ranch."

"The ranch he gave up for you?" her mother asked. "You do something crazy like that when you love someone so much they come first."

"There's that responsibility thing again," Norah said, frowning. "Putting me first. Everything for me, right? He wants me to have 'everything I deserve.' Except for him."

"Coming through," called a male voice.

Norah glanced up at her handsome brother-in-law, Liam Mercer, walking into the kitchen, an adorable toddler holding each of his hands. Despite being in the terrible twos, Norah's nephews, Shane and Alexander, were a lot of fun to be around.

Liam greeted everyone, then wrapped his wife in a hug and dipped her for a kiss, paying no mind to the flour covering her apron. Norah's heart squeezed in her chest as it always did when she witnessed how in love the Mercers were.

You should hold out for that, she told herself. *For a man who loves you like Liam loves Shelby. Like Dad loved Mom.*

Like I love Reed, she thought with a wistful sigh.

In just a few hours he'd be at the ranch, which they'd both have to give up, and the wonderful way he was with the triplets would tear her heart in two. She could have everything she'd ever wanted if Reed would just let go of all those old memories keeping him from opening his heart.

Hmm, she thought. Since being around the triplets did have Reed Barelli all mushy-gushy and as close to his feelings as he could get, maybe she could do a little investigative detective work of her own to see if those "feelings" he spoke of having for her did reach into the recesses of his heart. She knew he wanted her—their night in Las Vegas had proved that, and she knew he cared for her. That was obvious and he'd said it straight-out. But could he enter into a romantic relationship with her and hold nothing back?

The man was so good at everything. Maybe she could get him to see that he could be great at love, too.

"Something smells amazing," Reed said when Norah opened the door. For a moment he was captivated by the woman herself. She wore jeans and a pale yellow tank top, her long, reddish-brown hair in a low ponytail, and couldn't possibly be sexier. His nose lifted at the mouth-watering aroma coming from somewhere nearby. "Steak?"

"On the grill with baked potatoes and asparagus at the ready."

"Can't wait. I'm starving." He set a large, brown paper bag down by the closet. "Where are the brand-new eight-month-olds?"

She smiled. "In their high chairs. They just ate."

"Perfect. It's party time." He trailed her into the kitchen carrying the bag. He set it on the kitchen table and pulled out three baby birthday hats, securing one on each baby's head.

"Omigod, the cutest," Norah said, reaching for her phone to take pictures. She got a bunch of great shots. Including Reed in several.

"For the eight-month-olds," Reed said, putting a chew rattle on Bea's tray. And one on Bella's and one on Brody's. "Oh, I set up a college fund for them today. And got them these new board books," he added, pulling out a bunch of brightly colored little hardcovers. At first he'd gone a little overboard in the store, putting three huge stuffed animals in his cart, clothing and all kinds of toys. Then he'd remembered it wasn't even their first birthday and put most of the stuff back.

"Thank you, Reed," she said. "From the bottom of my heart, thank you. I can't tell you how much it means to me that they're so special to you."

"They're very special to me. And so are you, Norah." With the babies occupied in their chairs with their new rattles, he moved closer to their mother and tilted up her chin. "I'm an idiot."

"Oh?" she asked. "Why is that?"

"Because I almost lost you to that French chef. Or any other guy. I almost lost you, Norah."

"What are you talking about? I'm alive." She waved a hand in front of herself.

"I mean I almost lost out on being with you. Really being with you."

"But I thought—"

"I couldn't get the triplets gifts and not get you something, too," he said. "This is for you." He handed her a little velvet box.

"What's this?" she asked.

"Open it."

She did—and gasped. The round diamond sparkled in the room. "It's a diamond ring. A very beautiful diamond ring."

He got down on one knee before her. "Norah, will you marry me? For real, this time? And sober?"

"But I thought—"

"That I didn't love you? I do. I love you very much. But I was an idiot and too afraid to let myself feel anything. Except these little guys here changed all that. They cracked my heart wide-open and I had to feel everything. Namely how very deeply in love with you I am."

She covered her mouth with her hands. "Yes. Yes. Yes. Yes."

He grinned and stood and slid the ring on her finger. "She said yes!" he shouted to the triplets, then picked her up and spun her around.

"I couldn't be happier," she said.

"Me, either. I get you. I get the triplets. And, hey, I get to live in the ranch because the owner is going to be my wife."

She smiled and kissed him and he felt every bit of her love for him.

"So the Luv U Wedding Chapel?" she asked. "That would be funny."

He shook his head. "I was thinking the Wedlock Creek Wedding Chapel."

Her mouth dropped open. "Wait. Are you forgetting the legend? You *want* more multiples?"

"Sure I do. I think five or six kids is just about perfect."

She laughed. "We really must be insane. But you'll

be in high demand to teach the multiples classes. You'll never have a minute to yourself."

"I'll be too busy with my multiples. And my wife."

"I love you, Reed."

"I love you, too."

After calling her mother, aunt and sister with the news—and Reed could hear the shrieks and cheers from a good distance away, Reed called Annie Potterowski at the chapel.

"So, Annie... Norah and I would like to book the chapel for an upcoming Saturday night for our wedding ceremony. We're thinking a month from now if there are any openings."

Now it was Annie's turn to shriek. "You're making your grandmother proud, Reed. How's the second Saturday in August? Six p.m.?"

"Perfect," he said. Norah had told him a month would be all she'd need to find a wedding dress and a baby tux for Brody and two bridesmaids' dresses for Bella and Bea. Her family was already all over the internet.

"And we'll spell our names right this time," he added.

A few hours later the triplets were in their cribs, the dishes were done and Reed was sitting with his fiancée on the sofa, stealing kisses and just staring at her, two glasses of celebratory champagne in front of them.

"To the legend of the Wedlock Creek chapel," he said, holding up his glass. "It brought me my family and changed my life forever."

Norah clinked his glass and grinned "To the chapel— and the very big family we're going to have."

He sealed that one with a very passionate kiss.

Epilogue

One year later

Reed stood in the nursery—the twins' nursery—marveling at tiny Dylan and Daniel. Five days ago Norah had given birth to the seven-pounders, Dylan four ounces bigger and three minutes older. Both had his dark hair and Norah's perfect nose, slate-blue eyes that could go Norah's hazel or his dark brown, and ten precious fingers and ten precious toes.

Norah was next door in the triplets' nursery, reading them their favorite bedtime story. Soon they'd be shifting to "big kid" beds, but at barely two years old they were still smack in the middle of toddlerhood. He smiled at the looks they'd gotten as they'd walked up and down Main

Street yesterday, Norah pushing the twins' stroller and him pushing the triplets'.

"How do you do it?" someone had asked.

"Love makes it easy," Reed had said. "But we have *a lot* of help."

They did. Norah's family and the Potterowskis had set up practically around-the-clock shifts of feeding them, doing laundry and entertaining the triplets the first couple of days the twins were home. Many of their students from the past year had also popped by with gifts and offers to babysit the triplets, couples eager to get some first-hand experience at handling multiples.

Even the Dirks had come by. David and a very pregnant Eden—expecting twins without having ever said "I do" at the Wedlock Creek chapel.

"I've got this," David had said, putting a gentle hand on his wife's belly. "I thought I'd be scared spitless, but watching you two and taking your class—easy peasy."

Reed had raised an eyebrow. David might be in for the rude awakening he'd been trying to avoid, but Reed wasn't about to burst his bubble. They'd have help just like the Barellis did. That was what family and friends and community were all about.

Norah came in then and stood next to him, putting her arm around him. "The triplets are asleep. Looks like these guys are close."

"Which means we have about an hour and a half to ourselves. Movie?"

She nodded. "*Jerry Maguire* is on tonight. Remember when we watched that?"

He would never forget. He put his arms around her

and rested his forehead against hers. "Did I ever tell you that you complete me?"

She shook her head. "You said it was nonsense."

"Didn't I tell you I was an idiot? You. Complete. Me. And so do they," he added, gesturing at the cribs. "And the ones in the room next door."

She reached up a hand to his cheek, her happy smile melting his heart. Then she kissed him and they tiptoed out of the nursery.

But Dylan was up twenty minutes later, then Daniel, and then the triplets were crying, and suddenly the movie would have to wait. Real life was a hell of a lot better, anyway.

* * * * *

Be sure to check out the first book in the
WYOMING MULTIPLES *miniseries:*

THE BABY SWITCH

Available now!
And look for Melissa Senate's next book, part of the
MONTANA MAVERICKS:
THE LONELYHEARTS RANCH *miniseries,*
THE MAVERICK'S BABY-IN-WAITING,
coming August 2018,
wherever Harlequin Special Edition books
and ebooks are sold.

Turn the page for a sneak peek at the latest entry in
New York Times *bestselling author*
RaeAnne Thayne's HAVEN POINT *series,*
THE COTTAGES ON SILVER BEACH,
the story of a disgraced FBI agent,
his best friend's sister and the loss that affected
the trajectory of both their lives,
available July 2018 wherever HQN books
and ebooks are sold!

CHAPTER ONE

SOMEONE WAS TRYING to bust into the cottages next door.

Only minutes earlier, Megan Hamilton had been minding her own business, sitting on her front porch, gazing out at the stars and enjoying the peculiar quiet sweetness of a late-May evening on Lake Haven. She had earned this moment of peace after working all day at the inn's front desk then spending the last four hours at her computer, editing photographs from Joe and Lucy White's 50th anniversary party the weekend before.

Her neck was sore, her shoulders tight, and she simply wanted to savor the purity of the evening with her dog at her feet. Her moment of Zen had lasted only sixty seconds before her little ancient pug Cyrus sat up, gazed out into the darkness and gave one small harrumphing noise before settling back down again to watch as a vehicle pulled up to the cottage next door.

Cyrus had become used to the comings and goings of their guests in the two years since he and Megan moved into the cottage after the inn's renovations were finished. She would venture to say her pudgy little dog seemed to actually enjoy the parade of strangers who invariably stopped to greet him.

The man next door wasn't aware of her presence,

though, or that of her little pug. He was too busy trying to work the finicky lock—not an easy feat as the task typically took two hands and one of his appeared to be attached to an arm tucked into a sling.

She should probably go help him. He was obviously struggling one-handed, unable to turn the key and twist the knob at the same time.

Beyond common courtesy, there was another compelling reason she should probably get off her porch swing and assist him. He was a guest of the inn, which meant he was yet one more responsibility on her shoulders. She knew the foibles of that door handle well, since she owned the door, the porch, the house and the land that it sat on, here at Silver Beach on Lake Haven, part of the extensive grounds of the Inn at Haven Point.

She didn't want to help him. She wanted to stay right here hidden in shadows, trying to pretend he wasn't there. Maybe this was all a bad dream and she wouldn't be stuck with him for the next three weeks.

Megan closed her eyes, wishing she could open them again and find the whole thing was a figment of her imagination.

Unfortunately, it was all entirely too real. Elliot Bailey. Living next door.

She didn't want him here. Stupid online bookings. If he had called in person about renting the cottage next to hers—one of five small, charming two-bedroom vacation rentals along the lakeshore—she might have been able to concoct some excuse.

With her imagination, surely she could have come up with something good. All the cottages were being painted. A plumbing issue meant none of them had water. The entire place had to be fumigated for tarantulas.

If she had spoken with him in person, she may have been able to concoct *some* excuse that would keep Elliot Bailey away. But he had used the inn's online reservation system and paid in full before she even realized who was moving in next door. Now she was stuck with him for three entire weeks.

She would have to make the best of it.

As he tried the door again, guilt poked at her. Even if she didn't want him here, she couldn't sit here when one of her guests needed help. It was rude, selfish and irresponsible. "Stay," she murmured to Cyrus, then stood up and made her way down the porch steps of Primrose Cottage and back up those of Cedarwood.

"May I help?"

At her words, Elliot whirled around, the fingers of his right hand flexing inside his sling as if reaching for a weapon. She had to hope he didn't have one. Maybe she should have thought of that before sneaking up on him.

Elliot was a decorated FBI agent and always exuded an air of cold danger, as if ready to strike at any moment. It was as much a part of him as his blue eyes.

His brother had shared the same eyes, but the similarities between them ended there. Wyatt's blue eyes had been warm, alive, brimming with personality. Elliot's were serious and solemn and always seemed to look at her as if she were some kind of alien life-form that had landed in his world.

Her heart gave a familiar pinch at the thought of

Wyatt and the fledgling dreams that had been taken away from her on a snowy road.

"Megan," he said, his voice as stiff and formal as if he were greeting J. Edgar Hoover himself. "I didn't see you."

"It's a dark evening and I'm easy to miss. I didn't mean to startle you."

In the yellow glow of the porch light, his features appeared lean and alert, like a hungry mountain lion. She could feel her muscles tense in response, a helpless doe caught unawares in an alpine meadow.

She adored the rest of the Bailey family. All of them, even linebacker-big Marshall. Why was Elliot the only one who made her so blasted nervous?

"May I help you?" she asked again. "This lock can be sticky. Usually it takes two hands, one to twist the key and the other to pull the door toward you."

"That could be an issue for the next three weeks." His voice seemed flat and she had the vague, somewhat disconcerting impression that he was tired. Elliot always seemed so invincible but now lines bracketed his mouth and his hair was uncharacteristically rumpled. It seemed so odd to see him as anything other than perfectly controlled.

Of course he was tired. The man had just driven in from Denver. Anybody would be exhausted after an eight-hour drive—especially when he was healing from an obvious injury and probably in pain.

What happened to his arm? She wanted to ask, but couldn't quite find the courage. It wasn't her business anyway. Elliot was a guest of her inn and deserved all the hospitality she offered to any guest—including whatever privacy he needed and help accessing the cottage he had paid in advance to rent.

"There is a trick," she told him. "If you pull the door slightly toward you first, then turn the key, you should be able to manage with one hand. If you have trouble again, you can find me or one of the staff to help you. I live next door."

The sound he made might have been a laugh or a scoff. She couldn't tell.

"Of course you do."

She frowned. What did that mean? With all the renovations to the inn after a devastating fire, she couldn't afford to pay for an overnight manager. It had seemed easier to move into one of the cottages so she could be close enough to step in if the front desk clerks had a problem in the middle of the night.

That's the only reason she was here. Elliot didn't need to respond to that information as if she was some loser who hadn't been able to fly far from the nest.

"We need someone on-site full-time to handle emergencies," she said stiffly. "Such as guests who can't open their doors by themselves."

"I am certainly not about to bother you or your staff every time I need to go in and out of my own rental unit. I'll figure something out."

His voice sounded tight, annoyed, and she tried to attribute it to travel weariness instead of that subtle disapproval she always seemed to feel emanating from him.

"I can help you this time at least." She inserted his key, exerted only a slight amount of pull on the door and heard the lock disengage. She pushed the door open and flipped on a light inside the cheery little two-bedroom cottage, with its small combined living-dining room and kitchen table set in front of the big windows overlooking the lake.

"Thank you for your help," he said, sounding a little less censorious.

"Anytime." She smiled her well-practiced, smooth, innkeeper smile. After a decade of running the twenty-room Inn at Haven Point on her own, she had become quite adept at exuding hospitality she was far from feeling.

"May I help you with your bags?"

He gave her a long, steady look that conveyed clearly what he thought of that offer. "I'm good. Thanks."

She shrugged. Stubborn man. Let him struggle. "Good night, then. If you need anything, you know where to find me."

"Yes. I do. Next door, apparently."

"That's right. Good night," she said again, then returned to her front porch, where she and Cyrus settled in to watch him pull a few things out of his vehicle and carry them inside.

She could have saved him a few trips up and down those steps, but clearly he wanted to cling to his own stubbornness instead. As usual, it was obvious he wanted nothing to do with her. Elliot tended to treat her as if she were a riddle he had no desire to solve.

Over the years, she had developed pretty good strategies for avoiding him at social gatherings, though it was a struggle. She had once been almost engaged to his younger brother. That alone would tend to link her to the Bailey family, but it wasn't the only tie between them. She counted his sisters, Wynona Bailey Emmett and Katrina Bailey Callahan, among her closest friends.

In fact, because of her connection to his sisters, she knew he was in town at least partly to attend a big after-the-fact reception to celebrate Katrina's wedding to Bowie Callahan, which had been a small destination event in Colombia several months earlier.

Megan had known Elliot for years. Though only five or six years older, somehow he had always seemed ancient to her, even when she was a girl—as if he belonged to some earlier generation. He was so serious all the time, like some sort of stuffy uncle who couldn't be bothered with youthful shenanigans.

Hey, you kids. Get off my lawn.

He'd probably never actually said those words, but she could clearly imagine them coming out of that incongruously sexy mouth.

He did love his family. She couldn't argue that. He watched out for his sisters and was close to his brother Marshall, the sheriff of Lake Haven County. He cherished his mother and made the long trip from Denver to Haven Point for every important Bailey event, several times a year.

Which also begged the question, why had he chosen to rent a cottage on the inn property instead of staying with one of his family members?

His mother and stepfather lived not far away and so did Marshall, Wynona and Katrina with their respective spouses. While Marshall's house was filled to the

brim with kids, Cade and Wyn had plenty of room and
Bowie and Katrina had a vast house on Serenity Har-
bor that would fit the entire Haven Point High School
football team, with room left over for the coaching staff
and a few cheerleaders.

Instead, Elliot had chosen to book this small, solitary
rental unit at the inn for three entire weeks.

Did his reasons have anything to do with that sling?
How had he been hurt? Did it have anything to do with
his work for the FBI?

None of her business, Megan reminded herself. He
was a guest at her inn, which meant she had an obliga-
tion to respect his privacy.

He came back to the vehicle for one more bag, something that looked the size of a laptop, which gave her
something else to consider. He had booked the cottage
for three weeks. Maybe he had taken a leave of absence
or something to work on another book.

She pulled Cyrus into her lap and rubbed behind
his ears as she considered the cottage next door and
the enigmatic man currently inhabiting it. Whoever
would have guessed that the stiff, humorless, focused
FBI agent could pen gripping true crime books in his
spare time? She would never admit it to Elliot, but she
found it utterly fascinating how his writing managed
to convey pathos and drama and even some lighter
moments.

True crime was definitely not her groove at all but
she had read his last bestseller in five hours, without so
much as stopping to take a bathroom break—and had
slept with her closet light on for weeks.

That still didn't mean she wanted him living next door. At this point, she couldn't do anything to change that. The only thing she could do was treat him with the same courtesy and respect she would any other guest at the inn.

No matter how difficult that might prove.

WHAT THE HELL was he doing here?

Elliot dragged his duffel to the larger of the cottage's two bedrooms, where a folding wood-framed luggage stand had been set out, ready for guests.

The cottage was tastefully decorated in what he termed Western chic—bold mission furniture, wood plank ceiling, colorful rugs on the floor. A river rock fireplace dominated the living room, probably perfect for those chilly evenings along the lakeshore.

Cedarwood Cottage seemed comfortable and welcoming, a good place for him to huddle over his laptop and pound out the last few chapters of the book that was overdue to his editor.

Even so, he could already tell this was a mistake.

Why the hell hadn't he just told his mother and Katrina he couldn't make it to the reception? He'd flown to Cartagena for the wedding three months earlier, after all. Surely that showed enough personal commitment to his baby sister's nuptials.

They would have protested but would have understood—and in the end it wouldn't have much mattered whether he made it home for the event or not. The reception wasn't about him, it was about Bowie and Katrina and the life they were building with Bowie's younger brother Milo and Kat's adopted daughter, Gabriella.

For his part, Elliot was quite sure he would have been better off if he had stayed holed up in his condo in Denver to finish the book, no matter how awkward things had become for him there. If he closed the blinds, ignored the doorbell and just hunkered down, he could have typed one-handed or even dictated the changes he needed to make. The whole thing would have been done in a week.

The manuscript wasn't the problem.

Elliot frowned, his head pounding in rhythm to each throbbing ache of his shoulder.

He was the problem—and he couldn't escape the mess he had created, no matter how far away from Denver he drove.

He struggled to unzip the duffel one-handed, then finally gave up and stuck his right arm out of the sling to help. His shoulder ached even more in response, not happy with being subjected to eight hours of driving only days postsurgery.

How was he going to explain the shoulder injury to his mother? He couldn't tell her he was recovering from a gunshot wound. Charlene had lost a son and husband in the line of duty and had seen both a daughter and her other son injured on the job.

And he certainly couldn't tell Marshall or Cade about all the trouble he was in. He was the model FBI agent, with the unblemished record.

Until now.

Unpacking took him all of five minutes, moving the

packing cubes into drawers, setting his toiletries in the bathroom, hanging the few dress shirts he had brought along. When he was done, he wandered back into the combined living room/kitchen.

The front wall was made almost entirely of windows, perfect for looking out and enjoying the spectacular view of Lake Haven during one of its most beautiful seasons, late spring, before the tourist horde descended.

On impulse, Elliot walked out onto the wide front porch. The night was chilly but the mingled scents of pine and cedar and lake intoxicated him. He drew fresh mountain air deep into his lungs.

This.

If he needed to look for a reason why he had been compelled to come home during his suspension and the investigation into his actions, he only had to think about what this view would look like in the morning, with the sun creeping over the mountains.

Lake Haven called to him like nowhere else on Earth—not just the stunning blue waters or the mountains that jutted out of them in jagged peaks but the calm, rhythmic lapping of the water against the shore, the ever-changing sky, the cry of wood ducks pedaling in for a landing.

He had spent his entire professional life digging into the worst aspects of the human condition, investigating cruelty and injustice and people with no moral conscience whatsoever. No matter what sort of muck he waded through, he had figured out early in his career at the FBI that he could keep that ugliness from touching the core of him with thoughts of Haven Point and the people he loved who called this place home.

He didn't visit as often as he would like. Between his job at the Denver field office and the six true crime books he had written, he didn't have much free time.

That all might be about to change. He might have more free time than he knew what to do with.

His shoulder throbbed again and he adjusted the sling, gazing out at the stars that had begun to sparkle above the lake.

After hitting rock bottom professionally, with his entire future at the FBI in doubt, where else would he come but home?

He sighed and turned to go back inside. As he did, he spotted the lights still gleaming at the cottage next door, with its blue trim and the porch swing overlooking the water.

She wasn't there now.

Megan Hamilton. Auburn hair, green eyes, a smile that always seemed soft and genuine to everyone else but him.

He drew in a breath, aware of a sharp little twinge of hunger deep in his gut.

When he booked the cottage, he hadn't really thought things through. He should have remembered that Megan and the Inn at Haven Point were a package deal. She owned the inn along with these picturesque little guest cottages on Silver Beach.

He had no idea she actually *lived* in one herself, though. If he had ever heard that little fact, he had forgotten it. Should he have remembered, he would have looked a little harder for a short-term rental property, rather than picking the most convenient lakeshore unit he had found.

Usually, Elliot did his best to avoid her. He wasn't sure why but Megan always left him...unsettled. It had been that way for ages, since long before he learned she and his younger brother had started dating.

He could still remember his shock when he came home for some event or other and saw her and Wyatt together. As in, together, together. Holding hands, sneaking the occasional kiss, giving each other secret smiles. Elliot had felt as if Wyatt had peppered him with buckshot.

He had tried to be happy for his younger brother, one of the most generous, helpful, loving people he'd ever known. Wyatt had been a genuinely good person and deserved to be happy with someone special.

Elliot had felt small and selfish for wishing that someone hadn't been Megan Hamilton.

Watching their glowing happiness together had been tough. He had stayed away for the four or five months they had been dating, though he tried to convince himself it hadn't been on purpose. Work had been demanding and he had been busy carving out his place in the Bureau. He had also started the research that would become his first book, looking into a long-forgotten Montana case from a century earlier where a man had wooed, then married, then killed three spinster school-teachers from back East for their life insurance money before finally being apprehended by a savvy local sheriff and the sister of one of the dead women.

The few times Elliot returned home during the time Megan had been dating his brother, he had been forced to endure family gatherings knowing she would be there, upsetting his equilibrium and stealing any peace he usually found here.

He couldn't let her do it to him this time.

Her porch light switched off a moment later and Elliot finally breathed a sigh of relief.

He would only be here three weeks. Twenty-one days. Despite the proximity of his cabin to hers, he likely wouldn't even see her much, other than at Katrina's reception.

She would be busy with the inn, with her photography, with her wide circle of friends, while he should be focused on finishing his manuscript and allowing his shoulder to heal—not to mention figuring out whether he would still have a career at the end of that time.

Don't miss THE COTTAGES ON SILVER BEACH
by RaeAnne Thayne,
available July 2018
wherever HQN books and ebooks are sold!

COMING NEXT MONTH FROM

HARLEQUIN®

SPECIAL EDITION

Available July 17, 2018

#2635 THE MAVERICK'S BABY-IN-WAITING
Montana Mavericks: The Lonelyhearts Ranch • by Melissa Senate
After dumping her cheating fiancé, mom-to-be Mikayla Brown is trying to start fresh—without a man!—but Jensen Jones is determined to pursue her. He's not ready to be a daddy...or is he?

#2636 ADDING UP TO FAMILY
Matchmaking Mamas • by Marie Ferrarella
When widowed rocket scientist Steve Holder needs a housekeeper who can help with his precocious ten-year-old, The Matchmaking Mamas know just who to call! But Becky Reynolds soon finds herself in over her head—and on the path to gaining a family!

#2637 SHOW ME A HERO
American Heroes • by Allison Leigh
When small-town cop Ali Templeton shows up at Grant Cooper's door with a baby she says is his niece, the air force vet turned thriller writer is surprised by more than the baby—there's an undeniable attraction to deal with, too. Can he be a hero for more than just the baby's sake? Or will Ali be left out in the cold once again?

#2638 THE BACHELOR'S BABY SURPRISE
Wilde Hearts • by Teri Wilson
After a bad breakup and a one-night stand, Evangeline Holly just wants to forget the whole thing. But it turns out Ryan Wilde is NYC's hottest bachelor, her new boss—and the father of her child!

#2639 HER LOST AND FOUND BABY
The Daycare Chronicles • by Tara Taylor Quinn
Tabitha Jones has teamed up with her food-truck-running neighbor, Johnny Brubaker, to travel to different cities to find her missing son. But as they get closer to bringing Jackson back, they have to decide if they really want their time together to come to an end...

#2640 HIGH COUNTRY COWGIRL
The Brands of Montana • by Joanna Sims
Bonita Delafuente has deferred her dreams to care for her mother. Is falling for Gabe Brand going to force her to choose between love and medical school? Or will her medical history make the choice for her?

YOU CAN FIND MORE INFORMATION ON UPCOMING HARLEQUIN® TITLES, FREE EXCERPTS AND MORE AT WWW.HARLEQUIN.COM.

HSECNM0718

SPECIAL EXCERPT FROM

H **HARLEQUIN**®

SPECIAL EDITION

*When small-town cop Ali Templeton finds the uncle
of an abandoned infant, she wasn't expecting a
famous author—or an undeniable attraction!*

*Read on for a sneak preview of
the next book in the AMERICAN HEROES miniseries,
SHOW ME A HERO,
by New York Times bestselling author Allison Leigh.*

"Are you going to ask when you can meet your niece?"

Grant grimaced. "You don't know that she's my niece.
You only think she is."

"It's a pretty good hunch," Ali continued. "If you're
willing to provide a DNA sample, we could know for
sure."

His DNA wouldn't prove squat, though he had no
intention of telling her that. Particularly now that they'd
become the focus of everyone inside the bar. The town
had a whopping population of 5,000. Maybe. It was
small, but that didn't mean there wasn't a chance he'd be
recognized. And the last thing he wanted was a rabid fan
showing up on his doorstep.

He'd had too much of that already. It was one of the
reasons he'd taken refuge at the ranch that his biological
grandparents had once owned. He'd picked it up for a
song when it was auctioned off years ago, but he hadn't
seriously entertained doing much of anything with it—
especially living there himself.

At the time, he'd just taken perverse pleasure in being able to buy up the place where he'd never been welcomed while they'd been alive.

Now it was in such bad disrepair that to stay there even temporarily, he'd been forced to make it habitable.

He wondered if Karen had stayed there, unbeknownst to him. If she was responsible for any of the graffiti or the holes in the walls.

He pushed away the thought and focused on the officer. "Ali. What's it short for?"

She hesitated, obviously caught off guard. "Alicia, but nobody ever calls me that." He'd been edging closer to the door, but she'd edged right along with him. "So, about that—"

Her first name hadn't been on the business card she'd left for him. "Ali fits you better than Alicia."

She gave him a look from beneath her just-from-bed sexy bangs. "Stop changing the subject, Mr. Cooper."

"Start talking about something else, then. Better yet—" he gestured toward the bar and Marty "—start doing the job you've gotta be getting paid for since I can't imagine you slinging drinks just for the hell of it."

Her eyes narrowed and her lips thinned. "Mr. Cooper—"

"G'night, Officer Ali." He pushed open the door and headed out into the night.

Don't miss
SHOW ME A HERO by Allison Leigh,
available August 2018 wherever
Harlequin® Special Edition books and ebooks are sold.

www.Harlequin.com

HSEEXP0718

LOVE
Harlequin
romance?

Join our Harlequin community to share your thoughts and connect with other romance readers!

Be the first to find out about promotions, news, and exclusive content!

Sign up for the Harlequin e-newsletter and download a free book from any series at

www.TryHarlequin.com

CONNECT WITH US AT:

Harlequin.com/Community

 Facebook.com/HarlequinBooks

Twitter.com/HarlequinBooks

Instagram.com/HarlequinBooks

Pinterest.com/HarlequinBooks

ReaderService.com

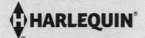 **HARLEQUIN®**

**ROMANCE WHEN
YOU NEED IT**

HSOCIAL2017

Reward the book lover in you!

Earn points from all your Harlequin book purchases from wherever you shop.

Turn your points into *FREE BOOKS* of your choice
OR
EXCLUSIVE GIFTS from your favorite authors or series.

Join for FREE today at
www.HarlequinMyRewards.com.

Harlequin My Rewards is a free program (no fees) without any commitments or obligations.

MYR17